7 SECRETS FOR SUCCESSFUL LIVING

7 SECRETS FOR SUCCESSFUL LIVING

TAPPING THE WISDOM OF
RALPH WALDO EMERSON
TO ACHIEVE LOVE, HAPPINESS,
AND SELF-RELIANCE

MARIANNE PARADY

Kensington Books

KENSINGTON BOOKS are published by

Kensington Publishing Corp.
850 Third Avenue
New York, NY 10022

Copyright © 1995 by Marianne Parady

Kensington and the K logo Reg. U.S. Pat. & TM Off.

ISBN 0-8217-5091-7

First Printing: October, 1995

Printed in the United States of America

To My Mother

With love and gratitude for the many blessings you
have brought into my life. Your loving heart,
continuous support, and generous nature have helped
make this book a reality.

ACKNOWLEDGMENTS

None of us travel alone. Throughout life's journey, helpmates appear to make the way smoother and the path clearer. Fortunately for me, many wonderful people have contributed to the publication of this book. Without them, it probably would not have been written. I'd like to thank them all.

To my dear and loving husband Bill, for his wisdom, insight, support, love, faith, and commitment, and for being "the love of my life."

To my mother, Antonette "Toni" Parady, to whom this book is dedicated, for her constant love and support. To Roz Costantino, my loving aunt, for being a lifetime source of inspiration and encouragement. To my brother David and sister-in-law Judy, for their generous gift of a computer when I couldn't afford to buy one; my brother Vic and my sister-in-law Kim, for their free help during tax season and for asking me to be Brielle's godmother, and my brother Jim, for his enthusiasm and support. To my nieces Brielle, Christina, and Kaylen, and my nephew David, for adding so much joy to my life.

To Helen Boyle, my mother-in-law, for her generosity in helping beautify my writing environment. To my sister-in-law, Susan Boyle Wood, and my brother-in-law, Dexter Wood, for their kind assistance with my computer.

To Gayle Fiabane, for her overwhelming encouragement, generosity, support, inspiration, and the use of her computer and office. To Cindy Zeleny, for her wisdom, support, and "oracle's" powers. To Pat Stezzi, for being a companion on the path. To Janie Fleisher, for her amazing intuition and insights. To Caroline Carmody, for her memorable cards, letters, and inspiring words. To Geraldine Lewis, for sharing the ups and the downs. To Liz Kemly, for her wondrous gifts of humor and wisdom. To M. Lynn Schiavi, for the "Salon" and for her faith in my book. To Geraldine Ackerman, for her unending help with the computer, from lessons to printing out.

To Meg North, for her valuable suggestions and infectious optimism. To Perle Besserman and Manfred Steger, for their insight and support. To Terry McNichol, for her ideas and for introducing me to Anthony DeMello. To Marilyn Funk, for her interest and for sharing the journey. To Laurie Morgente, for always seeing the "real me." To Ginny Panik, for her inspiring revelations. To Nese Venza, for her tee-hees and for giving me Thoreau's "castles in the air" quote in calligraphy. To Audree Kiesel, for her enthusiasm and interest. To Sandy Gay, for helping expand my horizons. And to Jack Hyle, for his help in "waking me up."

To Jacques and Ellen Duvoisin, for graciously offering their printer and fax machines. To Madeleine Ryan, for her accurate and timely readings. To Lea Wagner, for her amazing predictions. To Asia, for inspiring faith in the future. To Dr. Lee Harrod, for giving me the opportunity to teach and for his confidence in me. To Frank and Cathy Stout, for keeping my car expenses down. For Eli Dimeff, for his help in opening the spiritual doorway and for his "mailings."

To my uncle and aunt, Bob and Peggy Parady, for caring about my career. To my cousin, Ann Barbadore, for caring and for her inspiring cards. To Lin Grensing, for her help in getting me started with my first article. To Sandy Gilbert, for her transformative teachings and insights. And to Rev. Gwen Gillespie, for her life-enhancing wisdom, her prayers, and for helping me connect with myself and with God.

To Cathy Lyons-Colletti, for her belief in my writing ability and for countless other gifts of the heart. To Bob Smith, for his encouragement and for giving me the chance to write. And to every other giving soul whose presence in my life has made this book possible.

To my present editor, Tracy Bernstein, for her exceptional editing skills and for helping me make this book "the best it can be." To my first editor, Beth Lieberman, for seeing the possibilities in this project. And to my agent, Denise Marcil, for her perseverance, integrity, and support.

To the many writers and spiritual teachers who have inspired and transformed me, especially Ralph Waldo Emerson and his life-enhancing philosophy.

And finally, to those two special people who have left my life, but who will always remain close to me in spirit: my father, for his love and for helping me "to see"; and to Nanny, for her life-long devotion and for inspiring me on to greater things.

I offer my heartfelt appreciation for the part each of these people played in helping me fulfill my dream. May God bless all of them!

Contents

7 SECRETS FOR SUCCESSFUL LIVING

Introduction

Born in Boston, Massachusetts, in May of 1803, Ralph Waldo Emerson lived a relatively uneventful life, during which he nonetheless changed the course of American thought. For although he may have entered our lives only briefly, usually in high school or college English classes, his philosophy of individual freedom and spiritual realization are part of the American consciousness, whether or not we know it.

Emerson wrote mainly essays and poetry, though his poetry gets little notice today and is considered mediocre by literary standards. He is known mostly for his first and second series of essays, which were published between the years 1840 and 1850. A stirring lecturer, Emerson defied convention with the ideas he expressed, which ran contrary to the popular thought of his time. Despite this, many thinking Americans responded to his philosophy and held him in great esteem. Oliver Wendell Holmes said of him, "What he taught others to be he was himself." Even his critics admired this man who practiced what he preached.

Emerson's father died when he was eight years old, leaving the family poor and dependent on others for charity. Though Emerson suffered health problems throughout childhood, and for much of his life, in spite of deprivation and illness he diligently pursued his studies, gaining entrance into Harvard in 1817.

After a studious but rather undistinguished scholarly stretch at Harvard, young Emerson embarked upon a teaching career between the years 1821–1825. He was continually frustrated by the pedagogy of his time, which he believed impeded real learning; instead of teaching students to think, the current instruction inhibited the learning process by repeatedly programming youths with archaic ideas. Emerson also believed tests to be a waste of time because they measured only memorized facts and encouraged superficial understanding. After a few years of teaching, Emerson realized that he could not change the system, so he chose to resign from the profession rather than compromise his integrity by working within a structure that opposed his beliefs.

Descended from a long line of ministers, he next chose to become one and was installed as pastor of the Unitarian Old Second Church in Boston in 1829. But once again he had difficulty reconciling his spiritual beliefs with the practices of a rigid organization.

During the same year that Emerson became a minister, he married Ellen Tucker, to whom he was greatly devoted. Their happiness didn't last long, however, for she died in 1831, at about the time he resigned from the ministry. Devastated by his wife's death, Emerson sailed for Europe and, while in England, formed a great friendship with Thomas Carlyle, who helped him clarify his philosophy. It was here that the seeds of Emerson's own ideas were planted, launching him into the career of writing and lecturing that greatly influenced American thought.

After returning to New England in 1833, Emerson settled in Concord, Massachusetts, where he became the chief spokesperson for transcendentalism, a philosophical movement which relied on intuition as the means to discover spiritual truth. Other great thinkers and writers flocked to Concord, gaining inspiration from and absorbing the ideas of this great man. Henry David Thoreau was one of Emerson's most famous associates, but the Concord of that time also hosted such great minds as

Nathaniel Hawthorne, Amos Bronson Alcott, Margaret Fuller, and W. E. Channing. In the midst of this fermenting philosophical mixture, Emerson married Lydia Jackson in 1835, and settled happily in Concord for the rest of his life.

His years there were not without their tragedies, however, for in 1842, at the age of six, Emerson's first son, Waldo, died of scarlatina. Although heartbroken, Emerson continued with his writing and lectures. About his tragedies and disappointments Emerson wrote, "I am defeated all the time, yet to victory am I born." Realizing that misfortune does not prohibit us from experiencing life's joy and fulfillment, Emerson gained strength and developed his character through the challenges of his life, thus becoming an inspiration and guide to all who suffer.

Influenced by Eastern thought, especially Hinduism, Emerson also drew from the ideas of Plato, Swedenborg, and the German romantics, such as Goethe. Using his intuition as a guide, he accepted only ideas that resonated with his innermost being. Much of his wisdom originated solely from this intuitional center, and became a great source of enlightenment for himself and others.

Emerson's philosophy descended from the forefathers of democracy who, in the previous century, had forged a new way of life, promising freedom and the pursuit of happiness for all. Emerson took up the torch of individualism and freedom, fired it with divine light and passed it on to many during the nineteenth century. It is my wish, as we approach the twenty-first, that he may pass it on to you.

For as long as I can remember, the pursuit of happiness and success has been the consuming passion of my life. As a child, I often wondered why most people seemed unhappy and rather bored, even though they followed all the "rules" laid down by God and man. If there is a God, I'd wonder, then why doesn't he show us how to be happy? I did notice, however, that some people did manage to live rather successfully, and thoroughly enjoyed the rich and varied pleasures of this earth.

Entranced by my limited perception of successful living, I determined, during those late adolescent years, to make success and happiness my goals and to do whatever I needed to achieve them. After all, society had already defined success as the acquisition of things, of pleasure, and of power—romantic love, money, position, valuable possessions, lavish homes, expensive cars, travel, etc. So with the socially accepted blueprint to guide me, I set out upon my life knowing that "with faith—and determination—all things are possible."

The road I traveled, much to my surprise, was a rather bumpy one and contained all sorts of derailments, as well as false prophets. Glamorous jobs that seemed to promise success would satisfy me for a while, but would always self-destruct, leaving me empty and more desperate for success. Each man I thought would save the day ultimately disappointed me.

Then I hit the jackpot, or so I thought. For at twenty-five years old, my prince finally came, married me, and whisked me off to a foreign land, where we began what I thought would be the greatest adventure of my life. Upon our return, success beckoned to both of us and we embraced it, netting for ourselves the lavish and glamorous life I had dreamed about as a child. By twenty-eight, I had finally arrived, the prosperous eighties blessing us with success and the fulfillment of American dream.

During those prosperous years, I discovered that dream has some holes in it. For though I had everything I'd ever wanted, I was still filled with discontent. Though successful by the world's standards, I felt empty inside and wondered along with Peggy Lee, Is that all there is?

But, that was not all, for soon afterward, failure wiped out our American dream. Divorce shattered the romantic illusion, leaving both of us strapped with debt and broken. While trying to put Humpty Dumpty back together again, I came upon Ralph Waldo Emerson's essays which started me on the real journey toward success and fulfillment.

First of all, I discovered a spiritual essence within myself, and within the world, that transformed me and my life. Through reading, self-exploration, and reflection, I learned that the source of happiness and success lies within ourselves, not within the outer world. And I found, in Emerson's essays, the guidance I needed to begin the greatest of all journeys—the journey to self, and to God.

Throughout this journey, which began eight years ago, I realized that what we as a nation call success is merely an illusion that can never bring us true happiness. What it can bring is comfort, ease, security, and momentary pleasure, which for many is enough. Yet there are those who want more out of life, who want to live fully. We want to glimpse the eternal and know God, ourselves, truth, and love. We also want to fulfill our potentials and our missions—and leave the world, as Emerson said, "a little bit better" than we found it.

During these seven years of exploration, I have come upon many books and teachings that promise one the world and everything in it. I have also come across many teachings that promise things "not of this world." And while I have gained much from every guide that has crossed my path, for me, Emerson combines the best of both of these worlds, for he weaves the spiritual and material worlds into a rich tapestry of profound wisdom, mystical revelation, and practical advice.

Since reading Emerson, I have remarked to many people that if we could only follow his ideas and philosophy, we would truly enjoy a happy and successful life. And so the impetus for 7 Secrets for Successful Living was born, in order to transfer to you the wonderful and life-altering guidance of one of America's greatest minds.

As many of us know, Emerson, who was a rather aristocratic gentleman of the nineteenth century, is rough reading. Yet hidden within his antiquated language are what I consider to be the secrets to living. So I have attempted to take some essential kernels of his wisdom and interpret them in a simplified and practical way—hence, the verb "tapping" in the subtitle. Obviously, I have added my own ideas, as well as those of others, in the hope of creating a modern day guidebook for living. This is not intended to be a scholarly work, but a work from my heart and mind, as well as from Emerson's.

And as for the validity of the principles outlined in the book, I can honestly say that following Emerson's ideas has totally transformed my life. For they have helped me find my essential self, the person I was meant to be from birth, and to develop that self to its greatest potential. As with any self-help book, how-

ever, one needs to integrate these principles within his or her
being, and live them daily. Unfortunately, this is easier said than
done, for it takes time and effort to undo programmed habits
and ways of living.

Furthermore, although I have benefitted greatly from these
new ideas, at times I still struggle with the human tendency to
self-doubt and frustration. In short, I too have a long way to go
to reach total fulfillment. But at least I now have the tools to
achieve it—and a map to show me the way to the bliss that
awaits us all.

These tools have enabled me to truly live successfully, which
entails cultivating *all* parts of our gardens, starting with our
roots. For the spiritual life provides the foundation for everything we are and everything we do. Realizing that God lives
within us, as well as within the world, helps us to grow spiritually, creatively, psychically, emotionally, physically, and even
materially. For Emerson's philosophy does not deny us the
things of the world; it only suggests that we put the things of the
spirit first.

In the past decade, many of us have learned this lesson after
discovering that society's version of success has left us wanting.
Frustrated and disillusioned with the American dream, we are
stepping out onto new trails, trying to find "that something"
that has been missing all along. In this unchartered territory, we
must discover our own paths to fulfillment, rather than accept
anyone else's. And although others can provide us with guide-
posts along the way, we must, if our lives are to have any value,
create our own blueprints for success and happiness.

My hope is that this book will provide you with some guide-
posts, which, if you let them, will help you create a truly successful life, a life as unique as you are.

Note: As was the convention in the nineteenth century and
before, Emerson used the word "man" to mean both men and
women. Since I did not want to alter his original writings, I left
them with "man" predominating throughout. Instead of human-
kind, you will see references to mankind, and instead of he or
she, the pronoun "he" is used to refer to both sexes, and so on.

Furthermore, I feel I need to explain the terms used for God in this book, both by myself and by Emerson. Because God is such an undefinable and ineffable concept, I have chosen to use various additional terms, such as Universe, Divine Energy, Divine Essence, and Infinite Intelligence, among others. Most of the time, however, I have used God, because it is the word most of us are familiar with. I hope that instead of causing confusion, these multiple terms will help us to expand our original idea of the ultimate mystery, as well as to transform our relationship with it.

· 1 ·

The First Secret
Develop Self-Reliance

Man is his own star, and the soul that can
Render an honest and a perfect man
Commands all light, all influence, all fate
Nothing to him falls early or too late.

> —Epilogue to Beaumont & Fletcher's *Honest Man's Fortune,*
> quoted by Emerson at the beginning of "Self-Reliance."

The time has come to reclaim ourselves and our lives. We each must discover our own star and make it shine throughout the world. For the world needs light and love now more than ever before. The increasing violence, fear, and despair point to only one thing—something is terribly wrong with the psyche of humanity.

Ralph Waldo Emerson understood the problem and offered the solution. He called it "self-reliance," and knew that those who possessed this intangible jewel would be builders rather than destroyers, peacemakers rather than fighters, and would be fulfilled rather than frustrated. Emerson saw self-reliance as the key to happiness and success; he envisioned a world where authority and power exist first and foremost within each of us, instead of within society.

Society generally means that externalized system of authority that consciously and unconsciously dictates the direction and behavior of our lives. We allude to it when we wonder what "they" will think or worry whether we will measure up to "their" standards on issues as diverse as how we wear our hair or how we speak to each other. Concerned with freeing us from our cultural prisons, Emerson encouraged us to think and act for ourselves.

The first "secret" provides the cornerstone for the other six, as well as for any self-improvement program. For we need self-reliance in order to explore and implement any new concept in our lives. Without it, we become prey to external authorities; with it, we discern and listen to our own thinking before we allow the thoughts of others to influence us.

The building blocks of Emerson's philosophy are individuality and self-actualization; the foundation, a realization of the divine presence within each of us. The result, I'm afraid we have yet to discover, for the self-reliant have been few in number. Throughout most of the world's history, society and religion have dictated the direction of our lives and we have followed like unsuspecting sheep. For too long, we have turned our eyes and ears away from ourselves and toward external authorities. The time has come to look within ourselves, to discover who we are, and to start rebuilding our lives; for by developing self-reliance, we will find our own ways. Only then will we become fulfilled individuals who can ultimately transform the world.

Be Who You Really Are

> I will so trust that what is deep is holy, that I will do strongly before the sun and the moon whatever inly rejoices me and the heart appoints.
>
> —"Self-Reliance"

A topic of many self-help and spiritual writers today is the false self, the face that most of us show to the outside world. This self, formed by our socialization processes, molded by our wounds, and crystallized by our experiences, creates our lives for us. Yet, there is another self, an authentic self, which though hidden and obscured, tugs at the consciousness and bids one to wake up and become who one really is.

Emerson is the champion of this authentic self. He calls us forth to self-discovery, asking us to look beneath the facade to the divine and magnificent essences of our true beings. He asks us to do the work we were meant to do, say the things our hearts want to say, and live the lives our souls long to live.

When we are self-reliant, we make choices and take action in ways that resonate with our inner beings. We give up concern over "appearances" and concentrate on expressing our own truth and our own light. We do not bind ourselves in destructive relationships and lifestyles. Strong and sure of itself, the authentic self bonds with people out of choice, rather than out of desperation. Because of this inner strength, we can give up all manipulation, game-playing, power plays, cruelty, and insincerity; for we know that playing host to these worldly foibles can only bring us unhappiness and inhibit our spiritual growth.

Developing self-reliance is not a license for selfish behavior. It does not foster or support blatant disregard of those who inhabit this world with us. On the contrary, it opens up our hearts and develops our souls, so that we can become the loving, caring individuals we were meant to be.

My grandmother was a prime example of a self-reliant yet considerate human being. An Italian immigrant who performed the valuable task of raising a family, she followed the dictates of her heart throughout her ninety-two years. For example, although her parents strongly disapproved, she left Italy while only in her teens to marry my grandfather, who was waiting for her in America. Always oblivious to "rules" and "standards," her security came from within herself and she always spoke the truth. Never cruel or selfish, she allowed her heart to open, making her one of the most loving human beings I have ever known.

As my grandmother understood, self-reliance is not about changing ourselves, it is about *becoming* ourselves. For underneath all of our woundedness lies a whole human being waiting to be realized. Ignoring or betraying this authentic self is what I believe is responsible for much of the sickness and cruelty in the world today, for what we are all really seeking is to discover ourselves. And by doing so, we uncover the divine energy that runs through each and every one of us. We are all up to the challenge, and we can begin right now, by living from our hearts, not from our fears.

Fear, Fear, and More Fear

We are afraid of truth, afraid of fortune, and afraid of each other.

—"Self-Reliance"

I've often wondered why more people don't reclaim themselves and live lives of self-reliance and authenticity. Although it appears that the benefits far outweigh the deficits, most of us continue looking to our parents or society or the church for guidelines and rules. It is as if something deep inside us prevents us from connecting with our true selves and expressing them in the world.

A keen observer of human nature, Emerson saw that fear, the great paralyzer of human endeavor and human potential, could prevent us from jumping into authenticity and into life. Instead of despairing, however, we can search for the causes of our fears in order to understand them and hopefully disempower them.

The first on Emerson's list of fears is the fear of truth. An honest look at what goes on in our own lives, as well as in the lives of others, reveals a deep-seated resistance to dealing with reality. Most of us live with illusion and denial. We hesitate to admit, to ourselves or to others, our problems and weaknesses or our hopes and dreams. We walk with blinders on and hope it will all "go away." Or else we endlessly focus on a problem without dealing with the qualities in ourselves that may have caused it.

During my past marriage, I saw only what I wanted to. While the debts and the drinking increased, I focused my attention on enjoying our surface success and continued to indulge my every whim. When friends and family suggested that my ex-husband and I were living a destructive lifestyle, I became defensive and denied the possibility. After a while, the debts became too large to ignore. Banks and creditors were demanding payment, while our relationship deteriorated in the face of continued self-abuse. In essence, years of overindulgence had caught up with us, leaving a heap of ruins at our feet. The mess was so bad that it forced me to look at myself, my lifestyle, and my consciousness. I then came face to face with my self-destructiveness and self-hatred, and vowed to change my life.

Because of that experience, and other less dramatic ones along the way, I learned one of life's greatest lessons: that which you ignore ultimately controls you. By finally choosing to face and accept the truth of my life, I could make changes that would alter my destiny.

Another type of truth we fear is universal truth. For centuries, certain religions and philosophies have concealed the truth of our being, as well as the spiritual laws that govern the Universe. Conscious of the deeper nature of things, Emerson believed that God existed within us, as well as throughout the Universe. This realization, if we accept it, changes our experience of who we are and of how we live our lives.

By recognizing our divine nature, we connect with the energy that animates all things. We immediately feel one with the world, rather than separate and isolated. I've experienced this at times—not as often as I'd like—and it's an incredible feeling. While existing in this state, a tremendous sense of power and love well up from deep inside me. Any sense of helplessness and separateness dissipates; my heart opens and my worries and fears evaporate. During these moments, I know that God and I are one.

For many of us, the possibility of divine union is frightening. It almost seems blasphemous to unite ourselves with God, yet this is what the mystics throughout the centuries have done. As a matter of fact, Christ encouraged us to do just that when he spoke of the kingdom of God within us and when he said, "I and the Father are one."

Trained in powerlessness and victimhood, the thought of self-reliance and empowerment seems an impossible task to many of us. The "mindset," which often covers up our fears, is understandable; in order to move beyond it, we must accept ourselves for having it. For by accepting our fear, we can, if we want to, take small incremental steps toward disempowering it. We must understand that it is normal to experience fear when we wander out of our "comfort zone," away from the familiar. By experiencing it more and more, however, we can create a new comfort zone of strength rather than weakness, and of self-reliance rather than passivity.

Teilhard de Chardin said, "We are not human beings having a spiritual experience. We are spiritual beings having a human experience." This truth, expressed by many since the beginning of time, needs to be understood, realized, embraced, and acted upon by everyone before our world can change from one of fear and desperation to one of love and abundance.

Yet it is fear that seems to drive us through life. As Emerson noted we are "afraid of fortune." When we speak of fortune, we refer to the circumstances and outcomes of our lives, or to fate, as it is commonly called. Fears rush to the surface when we contemplate our individual destinies. We worry: What if I lose my job, or What if my spouse leaves me? We torment ourselves with future terrors: What if I don't have enough money for retirement? My God, I'll become a street person, or even worse. Or we cling to what we have: I'll be all alone in my old age if this relationship doesn't work out. Sound familiar? It does to me. John Bradshaw calls this process "catastrophizing," the perfect term for this great American pastime.

Catastrophizing, debilitating in itself, also reveals a rather untrustworthy attitude toward life and toward God. When I engage in this exhausting activity, my husband—a uniquely spiritual fellow—tries to tell me that I must have faith in life. "Faith in life," I bellow, "but what about . . ." "Life is always moving us toward greater degrees of wholeness," he explains. At this point, I either sheepishly agree or continue on with my list of future and past disasters.

After my mind returns to its normal state, I realize the truth of his statement. For whether through suffering or bliss, the events of my life have helped me heal and become more whole. This "wholeness," spawned through my difficulties, eventually added to my happiness and fulfillment. The irony of this rather strange phenomenon is that in a world of mostly religious people, too many of us are sorely lacking in faith.

Do we believe in a punitive God who likes to see us suffer or a loving God who wants us to be happy? If the latter, then these fears and worries about the future should have no power over us.

Obviously, suffering is part of life and should not be ignored. Yet our fears about it, and expectations of it, border on obsession at times. One of the reasons for this is that somewhere along the line, most of us have swallowed the idea of a punishing God who sends us hardship and pain. Why else would we live this way, anticipating all the terrors of the Universe?

A shift in consciousness is necessary. We need to believe that God *wants* us to be happy and fulfilled. We also need to meditate upon God's presence within us and feel its love in all its splendor. Then, we will look at the present and the future with faith, knowing that the Universe is friendly and that it wants us to fulfill ourselves on Earth so that we can be perfect expressions of Divine Energy.

To complete this discussion of our greatest fears, consider the fear Emerson says we have of each other. One of my favorite old movies is *Love Letters,* produced by David O. Selznick of *Gone With the Wind* fame. The screenplay was written by none other than Ayn Rand. In this film, Jennifer Jones's character tells Joseph Cotten about the good having amnesia has brought to her life. Sensing his confusion, she explains that she can now be completely herself because she has lost her fear of people along with her memory.

That line always stirs up my gut, because I have been afraid of people most of my life. What will they think of me? Will they like me? What if I say this and they get mad or think I'm weird or even hate me? Will they hurt me or leave me? Ugh . . . ! No wonder Emerson and self-reliance appealed to me so much.

An interesting concept, this fear of people. I've often thought when I'm dead and gone it won't matter a frog's navel whether anyone liked me or not. What will matter is whether or not I lived true to myself. What will also matter is whether I'd done my work and fulfilled my inherent purpose. When one looks at life *this* way, self-reliance becomes the only answer.

Until we reach that point, however, we can alleviate some fear by accepting ourselves for having it and then by understanding and acknowledging that we are all connected on some level.

Emerson believed that we all shared in what he called "the Over-Soul," or the soul of the Universe. In other words, each of our souls is part of this one great soul, which is ultimately God. Most of our fear of each other is engendered by our feelings of isolation and separateness. If we believed that each person contained the same soul as is within us, we would feel at one with others, rather than separate. This sense of "oneness" would make everyone a part of us, rather than a disconnected stranger. All would be "one of us," so to speak, instead of "one of them." Fears would dissipate, for we'd feel truly part of the human family.

In the PBS series, *The Power of Myth,* Joseph Campbell asserts that we could not relate to something totally separate from us. In other words, we are able to communicate with other human beings because we all share in this oneness. Carl Jung also believed we all share in what he called the "collective unconscious," a vast storehouse of universal consciousness, of which our individual consciousnesses are a part. When we understand this, we can truly view our fellow humans as brothers and sisters of the spirit, and know that many of our fears are unfounded.

As we begin understanding our unity with all that is, and move toward developing a strong foundation of self-reliance within ourselves, our fears will be transformed into guardians, who will guide us toward a magnificent and fulfilling future. When this happens, love will replace fear, and we will interact with our world as part of its harmony, rather than its dissonance.

Approval Seeking: Our Psychic Plague

> What I must do is all that concerns me, not what people think.
>
> —"Self-Reliance"

On a recent Oprah Winfrey show, a sixteen-year-old girl explained why she stayed with her boyfriend, even though he beat and abused her. "He was my whole world," responded the young woman, tears filling her eyes. "I thought that if I tried to make him happy, I would eventually be happy too."

The audience—and of course, Oprah—was shocked. How could this beautiful, intelligent young girl allow this to happen? Yet, if we look honestly at our lives, and at our socialization, we understand only too well how this and a thousand other abominations could, and do, happen.

Emerson wrote about the dangers of looking to others for approval and validation. Yet in our day, as in his, we are programmed to look to others for our sense of self-worth and dignity. This tendency, rooted deep within us, leads people away from themselves and toward lives and behaviors foreign to their individual needs and proclivities, causing low self-esteem and eventually self-hatred. And when we hate ourselves, we allow people to inflict all kinds of abuse upon us, because we unconsciously feel we deserve it. Then, in the proverbial vicious circle, we try even harder to gain others' approval, all the while neglecting ourselves and falling deeper into the abyss of total self-denial.

Emerson understood that the approval-seeking behavior most of us engage in leads to a betrayal so great that we slowly kill our real selves in the process. This insidious and unrecognized situation ruins more lives than we can ever imagine. Shakespeare, as did others before him, knew the cardinal rule of existence: "this above all, to thine own self be true."

Self-betrayal may begin with something as insignificant as wearing the same clothes as the rest of the crowd rather than what we really prefer. We may find ourselves dating people—or worse yet, marrying—to "look good," to gain attention and approval. Our career choice may also originate from a desire to please others or to be accepted, even though it may go against our natural inclinations. The possibilities are endless, as one self-betrayal leads to another, eventually leading us to a point where our real selves are almost nonexistent.

Furthermore, what we do to *ourselves* is usually done to us by others. When I look back upon my life, I can see that when I wasn't being true to myself, others were more likely to be untrue to me. I don't know why it seems to work this way, but years of experience have shown me the validity of this law.

During my mid and late twenties, I experienced more betrayal by others than I do now. For example, certain "friends" said and did things to hurt me behind my back, while some of my lovers strayed from monogamy. Increased self-realization has helped me to understand that during those tumultuous years, I wore a mask, and lived according to the persona I thought would serve me best in the world. The real me was hidden beneath this facade, trying to get my attention, but I denied and ignored its pleadings.

After total personal and financial collapse, I finally tore off the mask and began the work of self-discovery. Determining my own path has opened me up to my self and has enabled me to share this self with the world. Now betrayals are virtually nonexistent, unless I again get caught up in my old approval-seeking behavior. If so, I accept my failings with the understanding that learning to look to yourself for approval takes work and a high level of commitment.

The rewards, however, are well worth the effort, for what we give ourselves is given to us by the Universe, which showers us with more love and approval than ever before. As pleasant as this is, we discover that it is the love and approval we give ourselves that really transforms us and enables us to live happy and fulfilled lives. Only then can we allow the love of others to touch us with its healing balm.

Conformity—The Roadblock to Self-Reliance

You will always find those who think they know what is your duty better than you know it. It is easy in the world to live after the world's opinion; it is easy in solitude to live after our own; but the great man is he who in the midst of the crowd keeps with perfect sweetness the independence of solitude.

—"Self-Reliance"

Over 100 years ago, Ralph Waldo Emerson envisioned an end to the conformity that inhibits many of us from living our own lives. Yet here we are, on the threshold of a new millennium, still conforming to whatever we believe society expects of us. Rather than forging our own way, we look to others to determine our dress, our homes, our thoughts, and our lifestyles. Although not necessarily "bad," living this way prevents us from discovering ourselves and developing our potential; for true potential can only emerge out of our true selves. Unfortunately, most of us lead lives that are mere imitations of what has gone before, or of what exists now, leaving us clueless as to what we really want or who we really are.

Often, we choose to marry and have a family because it is what society—or our family or religion—expects of us. We may not be aware of these influences, hidden deep within our psyches, which cause us to take this step before we are ready. I've often been startled at the blank looks I get when I ask certain people why they married or had a family. In many cases, they just don't know. From others I hear, "It just seemed like the thing to do." Of course, there are those who have thought long and hard about these important decisions and have understood their motivations.

Even in today's "liberated" world, unmarried women—and men—over thirty are still looked at rather suspiciously. I still hear people say of singles in their thirties and forties, "There must be something wrong with them." I've often been tempted to respond by noting all of the "married" people I know who lead less than stable lives.

The truth is, not everyone is designed for marriage or child-rearing, just as everyone is not designed to work nine to five. If more of us followed our own hearts, perhaps we would have fewer abused children and fewer frustrated employees.

When we ignore our own leanings, we have very little to give to anyone, especially society. A frustrated accountant, who is really a painter at heart, will benefit society more if he does that which he is meant to do. Any choice, career or otherwise, that is not from the heart breeds nothing but futility and mediocrity. Just look at the world today and you can see the truth of this statement in the unfulfilled lives of most of its inhabitants.

Self-reliance can be achieved by all of us. Unfortunately, only a few have the courage and foresight to really live their lives. Ironically, these "few" are often the ones we elevate to "celebrity status" and seek to emulate. Paradoxically, the same society that pressures you and me to behave a certain way has turned people like Madonna and Michael Jackson into veritable gods. And believe me, you can't get much more individual than these two paragons of nonconformity.

If we look at "celebrities," we can see that the self-reliance and nonconforming ways of some have enabled them to enjoy fame and fortune. This amusing paradox shows an underside to our conformist society; one that encourages conformity on the one hand, yet admires and deifies nonconformity on the other. I believe this occurs because deep within we admire true individuality, while superficially we fear and despise it.

The roots of our nation were put down by individuals, not by conformists. Their independence lies within us, encouraging us to follow their lead. Fortunately, more and more people today are striking out on their own. If we join these self-reliant individuals, we may reach the heights those before us have attained, or we may just possess that rarest and most precious of things—ourselves.

The Danger of "Reactive" Nonconformity

> Good and bad are but names very readily transferable to that or this; the only right is what is after my constitution, the only wrong what is against it.
>
> —"Self-Reliance"

During the sixties and seventies, the youth of America waved the banner of nonconformity and waged war against everything they labeled "Establishment." Emerson and Thoreau were rediscovered during this era, helping to set the stage for a social revolution destined to change the world. But not much happened. The valiant ideals and egalitarian reforms amounted to little more than a flash in the pan, leaving the way open for the conservatism and materialism of the Reagan era.

Although the ideals of this period were powerful, somehow they just didn't take hold. Society needed reform, and here were the reformers; but something backfired and almost returned us to the narrow confines of the fifties, with its strict moral codes and emphasis on appearances.

In the book, *Your Mythic Journey*, Sam Keen and Anne Valley-Fox explain that "when being *against* becomes more important than being *with* or *for*, the enemy has destroyed the independence of your personality." This profound statement sheds light on what went wrong with the nonconformity of the 1960s: it was more a reaction *against* something than a movement *toward* something else. For when we fight against something or someone, our focus is on our enemy rather than on our goals. This type of misdirected concentration gives the enemy incredible power over us, for if they were not so powerful, we wouldn't need to fight so hard.

When we concentrate more on what we *don't* want than on what we *do*, we place the enemy in a position of control, where he/she/it can slowly drain our energy and eventually triumph over us. What usually happens in these cases is that the enemy occupies a place within us, as well as without. The power we give it allows it to grow, usually unobserved, within ourselves and inevitably beats us at our own game.

During most of my youth, I rebelled against my parents by avoiding anything that smacked of middle-class values. To me, a government or corporate job, marriage to a nice, average guy, a home in the suburbs, and station wagons represented conformity and a total denial of individuality. Instead, I wanted a life of money, privilege, excitement, and luxury, one in which I could live by my impulses and make my own rules. And although conformity existed in this lifestyle as well, it was not the middle-class conformity I was battling against.

After my awakening to this, I also realized that my war against conformity contained a great deal of fear—fear of that which I thought would drain me of my life. Frightened of losing my individuality and "spirit," I fought long and hard against any system, family or otherwise, that threatened my sense of self. In reality, however, a part of me feared the truth of all I fought against; perhaps "they" were right, I thought in secret terror. My "enemy" had me by the tail and I was futilely chasing after it. After I made peace with this conflicting part of myself, I decided to live from my truth, rather than strive for nonconformity. For reactive nonconformity contains the same ingredients as conformity does, namely an absence of true inner power and faith in one's self.

When striving for independence and self-reliance, one's impulses need to come from desire for a certain type of life, rather than from the repulsion of another. If they don't, our repulsion will end up disempowering us and may prevent us from achieving our desires.

Conformity Drains Power

> He who knows that power is inborn, that he is weak because he has looked for good out of himself and elsewhere, and so perceiving, throws himself unhesitatingly on his thought, instantly rights himself, stands in the erect position, commands his limbs, works miracles.
>
> —"Self-Reliance"

When we think of power, we usually think of money, position, physical strength, and other external sources. When Emerson speaks of power, however, he speaks of an inner source of empowerment by which we become the heros of our own lives, rather than victims. This power has nothing at all to do with external situations, but everything to do with our connection to God. This connection imbues us with divine energy, which generates authentic power, thereby helping us move confidently toward self-fulfillment and self-actualization.

We cannot be truly powerful unless we live from the truth within ourselves. Jesus is an example of someone who lived from this truth, which might explain why his influence is so great. When we have this kind of "power," we sit at the helm, steering our lives into a congruence with the deepest truth of our beings.

This life needn't be grand, or full of the trappings of fame or fortune. It requires only that you work at a job that truly represents who you really are, communicate honestly, and engage in a lifestyle that reflects your inner world. When we live this way, we fill ourselves with the power of the Universe, which is love.

Conforming to a way of life you do not believe in diminishes your power, for you are working against yourself. Although you may accomplish much in the way of outward success, in your core fear and weakness reign. Why do you think many people feel disillusioned when they finally achieve success? Those who do usually say "something is missing," and that something is usually their real selves.

In Emerson's terms, self-reliance is the key to authentic power. For within ourselves lies the very energy of the Universe, which can only be tapped by congruent living, in which what we say and do accurately reflects our inner life.

To clarify this point further, try to remember a time when you were talking to people with whom you didn't agree. If you nodded and affirmed their opinions, fearing their disapproval and possible rejection, you probably experienced a power drain. This could be felt by a shift in your energy level, perhaps by a sick feeling in your gut, or by a change in the vitality of your voice.

When I am in this type of situation and don't stay true to myself, I notice my voice becoming shaky and slipping into a monotone. Instead of an inner feeling of strength and confidence, I experience a sense of weakness as my self-esteem is depleted.

On the other hand, when I speak from *my* truth and don't allow others to intimidate me, I notice a freedom emanating from within me as my inner power increases. Rather than condemning those with different opinions, I find that when I am empowered, I welcome the differences and enjoy engaging in frank and hearty discussions. When we are truly empowered, we encourage everyone to think in his or her own way, rather than trying to change others.

Free at Last

Nothing can bring you peace but yourself.

—"Self-Reliance"

One of the end results of following Emerson's philosophy of self-reliance is liberation from what he calls the "wheel of fortune," which represents the ups and downs of our lives. While riding on this "wheel," we are happy when something good happens and sad when something bad happens. In other words, we let the circumstances of our lives control our states of mind and determine how we react.

To illustrate, let's say you've finally met the man or woman of your dreams and you are ecstatic. Happiness pervades your days and sorrow is forgotten. But just let that person leave you and what happens? Happiness becomes sadness and the wheel rolls on.

Now, I realize that this is the way we have been programmed. The human tendency to believe happiness depends on people and circumstances is well documented and universal. Buddha called it "attachment" and saw it as the root of all sorrow.

Self-reliance weans us away from attachment by changing our source of happiness from that without to that within. Now we create our own happiness rather than waiting for outside stimuli to affect us. This way of life is the "living from your center" that Joseph Campbell talks about.

Living self-reliantly and without attachment does not mean that we are unaffected by adversity, or that we repress or suppress emotions. Remember, the root of self-reliance is being true to oneself, which discourages any sort of repression. The difference is, when we are truly living from within, we feel connected with an inner reservoir of strength, which allows us to weather the difficulties of life with equanimity.

When we live this way, we may experience all the same emotions as before, but they lose their power to unsettle and weaken us. For we now bow to a new authority, the central core of our being, which is pure Universal Energy, or God. Emerson's philosophy focuses our attention away from the things of the world, and toward the God within.

Our world encourages us to look without for our security, our happiness, and even our God. Our own society's preoccupation with "success" and material things reveals something lacking deep within our national psyche.

We have all known people—or perhaps it is ourselves—who have an insatiable need to acquire more and more material goods. It is as if there were a gaping hole inside that can never be filled. I spent about five years living this way; the phrase "shop till you drop," was probably coined just for me. I can remember actually counting the items I possessed in the hope of filling a void and building my self-esteem. Unfortunately, my purchases only temporarily soothed me, but did nothing to heal me.

As I began to heal myself, a sense of wholeness emerged from the same place where the hole had been. Gradually, I lost my need to shop incessantly, and I now enjoy shopping as a choice, not a compulsion.

Material things—love, food, drink, knowledge, or anything else that makes the world more pleasurable and comfortable—are meant to be enjoyed. The irony is, we can only enjoy them when we have let go of our attachment to them. For when we are attached, we live in fear of losing that which we desire, and are never completely free to enjoy it fully.

For example, let's say that you're attached to the love relationship in your life. You believe you'd die without it. Locked in this state of mind, you find that fear nudges you often. Although barely noticeable at first, as the relationship goes on and the attachment grows, jealousies and doubts start to arise. You then may torture yourself with "what ifs," and spend many of your waking—and sleeping—moments obsessing over losing this person. At this point, you aren't free to enjoy the beauty of the relationship and may even strangle it with your clinging and fear.

Although the previous example is more the norm than the exception, we do have the power to engage in relationships that originate from love rather than fear. When we develop self-reliance, we loosen our hold on the world and finally are able to enjoy its fruits and its beauties without the terror of loss.

Self-reliance can also point the way to the wholeness within us. When we accept the fact that deep within we are complete, not fragmented, our view of life changes. Our needs and dependencies then change to wants, which we can freely choose to satisfy or not. When we look to the outside for completion, however, a sense of lack clings to us no matter where we go.

If we let it, Emerson's philosophy of self-reliance can open us up to the world and the world to us. It can help us to realize our wholeness and to live from that instead of from fragmentation. When that happens, our lives will take on new meaning as we move courageously through their many challenges.

Society's Resistance to Self-Reliance

It is easy to see that a greater self-reliance must work a revolution in all the offices and relations of men; in their religion; in their education; in their pursuits; their modes of living; their association; in their property; in their speculative views.

—"Self-Reliance"

The bottom line is that self-reliant individuals are happier, more fulfilled, and more productive members of society than their dependent counterparts. But if this is true, why doesn't society encourage us to become the independent thinkers we were meant to be?

Emerson pondered this dilemma and came to the conclusion that our whole way of life would have to change if we spawned a nation of self-reliant and free individuals. Sensing an unspoken conspiracy operating, he believed that society discourages self-reliance, even though it may seem, on the surface, to support it.

If we truly lived self-reliantly, we would produce a nation of independent thinkers. And independent thinkers could not be controlled as easily. This would disrupt what some see as the status quo, and would cause us to reexamine our ways of living.

Just imagine if we all spoke the truth at all times—this does not mean being cruel or inconsiderate, just honest. All manipulations and game-playing would cease, since authentic communication would be the rule. My, would this change the status of our relationships, especially the romantic ones, and create a new mode of loving and of marriage!

Certain abusive behavior and criminal acts would cease because fulfilled individuals are free of frustration, rage, and resentment. After all, much of our anger is bred from oppression, repression, and from not being true to ourselves. Believe me, self-actualized men and women have little desire to abuse or overpower anyone.

I could go on painting this seemingly idealistic picture of a self-reliant society, but will let your imaginations do the rest. In my mind, I can clearly see that a kinder, more loving world would emerge. Opponents of self-reliance believe anarchy would result, but I disagree. I'd rather have people expressing their impulses and leanings, not repressing them. For anything repressed eventually resurfaces in distorted and much more damaging ways. Why do you think countries like Germany and Holland have a significantly lower sexual abuse rate than we do here in the United States? I believe it is because they have an open, accepting view of sexuality, which they consider a very natural part of life.

When presenting these ideas to my classes (which are usually made up of eighteen- and nineteen-year-olds), I often ask them if they think it is easier to live self-reliantly or according to the dictates of society. Almost always, I get the same answer: it is *easier* to live as society determines than to follow your own heart.

If we accept Emerson's theory about society discouraging self-reliance, we can understand why my students believe as they do. For they are products of that same society that would rather breed followers than leaders.

Unfortunately, this truth is all too evident if we look around us. Because we have neglected the development of the self, we are drowning in a sea of neuroses, psychoses, despair, depression, and frustration. Our souls and spirits are sick and in need of care, and we must administer the treatment, first to ourselves and then to the world.

One Step at a Time

Nothing is at last sacred but the integrity of your own mind.

—"Self-Reliance"

When I first met with Emerson's profound ideas on self-reliance, I was overwhelmed by how far I had to go. Like most of us, I had allowed other people to affect my life more than I liked to admit. On the outside, I appeared independent and self-directing, yet on the inside I was bruised and shamed by others' never-ending judgments on my life and myself. After reading "Self-Reliance," I knew it was possible to value only *one's own* opinion of one's self, and to direct one's life in affirmative rather than rebellious ways.

Initially, I hated myself because of what I saw as my "wimpy" behavior. Self-reliance seemed a dream of freedom I was unlikely ever to attain. Then I discovered what Theodore Isaac Rubin meant when he said "Compassion for myself is the most power-ful healer of them all." I understood that by treating myself with compassion, I would be able to move toward my goal of self-reliance without bruising myself any further. After all, the last thing we need to do is judge ourselves as others have judged us.

After I looked at myself with compassionate eyes, I saw that I already had some qualities of self-reliance within me. They had always enabled me to maintain some semblance of my own life, in spite of the advice thrown in my way. I praised myself for these qualities and used them to enhance and increase my self-reliance in many ways.

For example, I learned to "just say no," when I didn't want to attend some function at which I felt obligated to appear. Before, I used to come up with excuses, such as "I've been throwing up all day, I can't possibly make it," or "My friend called and she's desperate, I must go to her instead." I changed this well-honed

technique to just saying "I'm sorry, I can't make it." No explanations, nothing, unless of course, I am asked, in which case I try to
answer honestly without being cruel. Remember, we are striving
for honest communication, not to hurt in any way. Obviously
when you live this way, some people may be hurt, but just think
of the hurt you do to your own integrity, and ultimately to other
people, when you feel you must fabricate in order to appease.

After each "honest" moment, I felt empowered and stronger
than ever before. If I did "wimp out," I noticed that I felt rather
sick in my gut. I soon realized that something in me couldn't live
dishonestly anymore, which caused me to honor my truth more
and more each day.

A bold move for me was to dissolve certain "friendships" that
existed more out of obligation than out of affiliation. Prior to
that time, I would just "go through the motions" of a friendship
that had run its course, afraid to speak the truth. Or, fearful of a
confrontation, I would avoid calling the person back or make
excuses for not getting together. When I finally decided to live
from truth, I wrote notes to certain people telling them I didn't
think we had enough affinity between us to remain friends. This
may seem cruel, and I'm sure it hurt them, but I couldn't visit
with them while knowing I didn't want to be there. That was an
insult to them, as well as a denial of my own truth. After all, how
many of us would want someone to spend time with us out of
obligation?

I also learned to make decisions about my life and my career
from my heart rather than from anyone's idea of what I "should
be doing." This was admittedly a struggle at times, especially
financially, but I couldn't have written this book if I hadn't
looked within and followed my own lead.

As my integrity grew, my life improved in ways I'd never
dreamed of. After a while, I found it hard to say anything I didn't
mean, or to do anything against my nature. I heard John Bradshaw once say that the more honest he becomes, the better his
life gets. I've found this to be true, as manipulation, flattery, and
game-playing have given way to authenticity. The payoffs have
been tremendous, and have included everything from a fulfilling
career to wonderful and cherished relationships.

When you commit to this way of living, it is important to begin with small steps, then gradually work your way up to the larger ones. For example, just saying what you really feel about something is a good place to start. It needn't be anything too controversial, you might just finally admit that you really like— or don't like—a certain kind of music. Don't move on to bolder subjects until you feel comfortable with the safer ones. Expect a bit of resistance at first, especially from those closest to you. Remember, we are all creatures of habit and don't like anything to change, especially the people we associate with.

After a while, you will realize that your inner power is fed by your new, self-reliant behavior and is diminished by your old dependent behavior. At this point, you'll find you can't go back to your old way of being. A new level of commitment will rise up within you, as life presents you with even greater challenges.

As with any other endeavor in life, mistakes will be made and slips will occur. When this happens, immediately forgive yourself and try to learn how to overcome the situation, should it occur again.

The statement "Many are called, but few are chosen" illustrates the rigors of the path of self-reliance, or the "hero's journey" as Joseph Campbell calls it. Difficulties will occur, but I can assure you that not living this way is ultimately more difficult in its wear and tear on the self. The "brass ring" of achievement, fulfillment, and joy awaits those who take up the challenge and follow their hearts. For they will discover their potential: intellectually, spiritually, creatively, materially, and emotionally. No price can be put on these treasures, which lie buried in the last place we would look—within ourselves.

· 2 ·

The Second Secret

*Develop a Relationship with the God
Within*

Abide in the simple and noble regions of thy life,
obey thy heart, and thou shalt reproduce the
Foreword again.

—"Self-Reliance"

In chapter one I introduced Emerson's belief that God exists
deep within us, in the center of our being. But stating this truth is
virtually useless; we must learn to experience this divine presence, and beyond that, develop a relationship with it. But how
do we begin? What we need, I'm afraid, is an experience of God,
rather than a creed. And this, my friends, is a bit more challenging than we might think. Fortunately, however, Emerson gives
us insights that may lead us toward that experience, and toward
developing what should be our primary relationship in life,
namely, our relationship with God.

The root of the word religion is *religio,* which means a linking
back to the source. Unfortunately, many of our religious institu-
tions lead us away from a direct connection with this source,
instead of toward one. By placing God outside us, they separate
us from the divine influx, rather than merge us with it. To heal
this split, Emerson's philosophy helps us link up again with the
source that exists within us and throughout the Universe. (In
fact, no real separation exists between the inner God and the
outer, for we are, in the deepest sense, one with everything and

everyone.) When we experience this "linking," our lives are transformed, and can never be the same again.

The First Step

Trust yourself—every heart vibrates to that iron string.
—"Self-Reliance"

Instead of asking us to accept a preconceived doctrine of belief, Emerson first asks us look within ourselves for truth. This concept of "looking within" threatens our social conditioning and defies our doubts, while opening up a whole new world of inner mystery and power.

Accustomed and trained to doubt ourselves, we look to outside authorities to tell us things we already know somewhere inside. Emerson believed that within us lies the means to all knowledge and that we only need to wake up and tap into this original intelligence. But how do we unearth this primary wisdom and receive the fruits of universal intelligence?

A leap of faith is necessary for the first step, which simply consists of this—trusting yourself. Emerson also asks us to trust that God is working through us and living within us. Unfortunately, it is our simple ignorance of this fact and our lack of trust that prevents us from living fulfilled and spiritually evolved lives.

Before we can connect with the divine part of our being, we must trust our inner promptings and dig for our own truth. We can begin this journey by listening to those inner messages that seem to compel us. For instance, suppose your "inner voice" tells you you need to spend some quiet time alone everyday. Or continually prompts you to go back to college? If these messages are truly coming from your intuition, following them is sure to enhance your spiritual growth and to bring you closer to the God within you. If you continue to follow these "hunches" on a daily basis, you will be well on your way to developing the most important relationship of your life.

Any relationship needs trust in order to flourish. This "inner" relationship is no different; it too needs trust in order to touch our lives with magic as only it can. For when we engage with the Divine within, the Divine engages with us and becomes our partner in life, rather than a stranger.

Goethe said, "As soon as you trust yourself, you will know how to live." When we don't trust ourselves, we often make decisions that may create unnecessary pain and obstacles for us. For example, a friend of mine entered law school despite the fact that her inner voice discouraged her. Because she didn't want to disappoint her family or look like a failure in front of her friends, she finished law school and became a lawyer, while hating it all the way. Eventually, she developed an ulcer and other physical problems while only in her twenties. Each time I talk to her, she tells me how uncomfortable and unhappy she is in her job and in her life. If she had trusted her inner voice's warnings, she could have saved herself much unhappiness and frustration.

One of the best ways to learn to trust yourself is to try it for a while and see what happens. Begin by trusting your thoughts, hunches, likes, dislikes, desires, passions, revelations, whatever. Trust what you think, not what others tell you to think. Even if what comes up seems strange to you, trust it anyway, especially if all your senses concur. Remember, Columbus was laughed at when he said the world was round. The majority can be wrong about anything!

Mistakes will inevitably occur as we attempt to sort through the myriad of voices that play on within us. Try to weed through them and focus on the ones that seem stronger and repeat themselves more than the others. Then put your trust into action by heeding these messages and see what happens. As you continue trusting yourself, note any changes occurring in your life. Also notice how self-trust makes you feel. Are you feeling more empowered and more at peace? Chances are, if you truly trust yourself—this doesn't mean an arrogant know-it-all attitude—your life will gradually transform itself into the lovely creation it was meant to be. For self-trust alters consciousness and consciousness alters a life.

To Trust or Not to Trust?

Let a Stoic open the resources of man, and tell men they are
not leaning willows, but can and must detach themselves;
that with the exercise of self-trust, new powers shall appear.

—"Self-Reliance"

As with most things that are good for us, we resist and sometimes persist in resisting. You'll probably find this true of self-
trust. Our "safety systems"—those parts of us that want
everything to stay the same—sense "change" and will fight to
prevent anything that will upset the status quo of our lives. So we
invent fears, which serve the purpose of keeping us "stuck" in
our old ways and our old life.

As mentioned in chapter one, we are afraid of our own power.
It is not worldly power, such as money, position, beauty,
strength, etc., that frightens us, but *authentic* power that makes
us quiver.

When we trust ourselves, and allow the Divine Energy into our
life, we cannot stay the same. Our lives must change when we
give up our role as victim, and take up our new role as an empowered being. One of the reasons we resist this evolution is
because of the losses that usually occur. For example, sometimes
certain friends drop out of our lives when they discover we are
dancing to a new tune. The gossiping and complaining stop
when we trust and empower ourselves, which leaves many silent
gaps in those old familiar conversations. Also, when we finally
decide to make that change, whether it be a new career, a new
relationship, or a new life, we discover that new responsibilities
appear that require us to organize our time in more productive
ways. The hours we spend on the phone may need to be replaced
by hours at the library, and endless shopping excursions may
give way to business trips that further our careers.

Unfortunately, we may find that certain people liked us better
when we were miserable. The old adage "misery loves company"

still holds true today. I know that when I began trusting myself, my previously thwarted goals and desires began to manifest, and I soon found that my life was better than ever before, which caused me to feel guilty with certain "friends" who were not as satisfied. At times, my guilt caused me purposely to create new problems in my life, just to generate the old "connection" again.

As I evolved, however, I realized that self-sabotage helped no one. It inhibited my spiritual growth, as well as kept my friends in their self-created prisons. After some soul-searching, I gradually became more comfortable with my "new" life, and understood that I could help others more by being an example, rather than being a companion in their futility.

Trusting yourself takes courage and a commitment to a better way of living. It also requires that you accept some discomfort with your emerging empowerment. Losses may also occur, but you will soon discover that any of these are replaced by greater and more expansive experiences, circumstances, and people, and that life just gets better and better. Take the chance and trust yourself; you and your life are worth it.

Intuition—God's Messenger

> Every man discriminates between the voluntary acts of his mind, and his involuntary perceptions, and knows that to his involuntary perceptions a perfect faith is due.
>
> —"Self-Reliance"

All this talk of trust inevitably brings us to the subject of intuition, which Emerson saw as God's messenger, the doorway to spiritual truth and to the truth of ourselves. Without it there is no relationship with the God within, for when intuition has shut down—or worse, has never been operative—the universal circuits are jammed, and divine messages cannot reach us.

Intuition plays only a small part in most of our lives, typically relegated to the "hunches" we get now and then, while our analytical and critical thinking skills get top billing. In Emerson's world, intuition is the primary vehicle for discerning truth of any kind. To him, all other thinking skills fall far behind this "primary wisdom."

He makes the distinction between "voluntary thoughts" and "involuntary perceptions," which seem to come from nowhere. They slip into consciousness via the heart and demand to be noticed. Emerson cautions us to pay attention to these messages, for they contain the very information we need to live a happy and a successful life.

For example, sometimes your intuition can point the way to a perfect career, as it did in my life. Since my late teens, my intuition relentlessly tormented me with desires for a writing career. The older I got, the stronger the messages became, and the more I tried to silence them. Afraid of true empowerment and self-exposure, I attempted to squelch those inner voices that knocked at my consciousness and told me "to write." So instead of following my intuition, I lost myself in a country-club existence, hoping that the social whirlwind would eliminate these bothersome messages. The truth is, it was not until my life fell apart at age thirty-one that I began to honor and to act upon this deep-seated desire.

But how can we tap our intuition? One of the first things we need to do is sort out the various voices that echo in our brains, producing contradictory and confusing messages which quite literally can drive us crazy! Obviously not all of these voices are intuitional, and following the wrong "voice" can lead us where we really don't want to go.

When you have a problem and you'd like to contact your intuition for guidance, first, block out a period of time—at least half an hour—when you can be alone. Use earplugs if you must, but find some silence and solitude. Then just sit quietly and meditate on your problem, allowing all the voices to come to the surface. Grab a piece of paper and write down each message—keep them separate, though. After you have written down all the messages, go back and see if you can identify where these voices are coming from.

For instance, one of the messages may be "Don't try that, you're sure to fail." Ask yourself if any individual or any group of people voiced a similar message to you at any time in your life.

If that occurred, then you know this message is probably not from your intuition. If you hear a message that considers other's opinions about you, such as "If I do this, they'll probably hate me" or "What will so-and-so think about this," you can pretty well assume that it is coming from that place in you that needs acceptance. In essence, any message that is based in fear, insecurity, self-doubt, self-hatred, or even self-aggrandizement is usually misdirected. After you have discounted the messages that seem to be from outside—or inside, though misdirected— sources, look at what you have left. In order to determine which remaining one is the intuitional solution, you will need to meditate on it.

In my own experience, when something comes from my intuition, my whole being feels empowered. But be careful here, for you might confuse empowerment with the "high" that usually accompanies something with an addictive edge to it. Similar to an adrenaline rush, this "high" is steeped in illusion, rather than based in reality. Like a drug-induced state, it is characterized by extreme bouts of euphoria out of proportion to the situation. Originating from our woundedness, this euphoric state seeks to re-create the world as we wished it to be during childhood when we believed in fairy tales and Santa Claus. To further clarify, compare the feelings of infatuation to those of love. Infatuation, much like alcohol, can send you to the moon, yet it often blows up in your face. Love, on the other hand, may not set off sky-rockets, but it can fill your whole being with a sense of joy and beauty unlike anything you have ever known. Like real love, the happiness generated from empowerment is peaceful, rather than frenetic. Its joy and power originate not from our woundedness, but from our wholeness, which is where our intuition resides.

After we "discover" what our intuitional choice is, then we must act upon it. (Remember the biblical saying "Faith without works is dead.") It is here that we really can determine the accuracy of our decision. Many times, the result will reveal to us that we followed the wrong voice. We can gauge this by determining whether our action ultimately enhanced our life or diminished it. Instead of fretting about the "wrong calls," welcome them as a way to distinguish between the different voices within us and to eventually discover our intuition.

An additional note on intuition and empowerment: if your decision leaves you feeling drained and low on energy, it is probably not from your intuition. Remember, intuition enlivens you because it is from your deepest soul. Another clue is that intuition usually creates a sense of coherence within us. Even though doubts may still creep in, your body, mind, emotions, and spirit seem to be united around this one "idea."

Unfortunately, nothing takes the place of good, old-fashioned practice; which means that the best way to develop your intuition is to follow it. Because of our "misprogramming," only consistent practice will net the greatest, and the most permanent, results.

Learning to hear and to trust your intuition is a challenging and often frustrating task. However, developing this skill can connect you with your own individual guidance systems and ultimately with God. By tapping into this universal intelligence, you can uncover the mysteries of your self and your life.

Sychronicity—The "Outside Connection"

> Oh believe, as thou livest, that every sound that is spoken over the round world, which thou oughtest to hear, will vibrate on thine ear! Every proverb, every book, every byword that belongs to thee for aid or comfort, shall surely come home through open and winding passages.
>
> —"The Over-Soul"

The preceding passage is an apt description of the process of synchronicity, which Carl Jung described as the "meaningful coincidences" of our lives. These are the events that, though seemingly unconnected, can provide us with guidance and direction. Great minds of the past, as well as the present, have formulated theories about synchronistic experiences, which seem to have an order and a purpose all their own. Emerson, as well, saw that the Universe worked with us and spoke to us through the outer world as well as from the inner world, and that it did so in both obvious and not-so-obvious ways.

Just as our intuition gives us answers and messages from within, synchronicity provides us with pertinent information from without. However, the key with synchronicity—and intuition, as well—is the correct interpretation of the message we receive.

A few years ago, I was driving along the Massachusetts turnpike with a friend, on the way to a relaxing weekend in New England, and I mentioned that I was going to choose a pen name for my writing career. Exactly at that moment, a car swerved into our lane, almost hitting us in the process. Startled, my friend and I looked at the license plate, which was right in front of us. Well, this startled us even more, for on the license plate was the name Parady.

As you know, I didn't change my name. This experience touched me on a soul level, providing me with one of the clearest examples of synchronicity. Within that situation, the possibility for misinterpreting the "message" was slim because the experience was so complete. Rather than interpreting the message with my mind, the truth of it resounded in the depths of my heart and throughout my being. A "gut" feeling—somehow, I just knew. No mental gyrations in progress, no wish fulfillment operating, no heavy analytical thinking involved. But this is not always the case.

I can remember one evening during my single years, when I met a charming Frenchman named Claude—name changed to protect the innocent. Sparks flew, as romance veiled both of us to reality. Toward the end of the evening, Claude informed me that he would be away on a business trip for two weeks, but he insisted we meet for dinner when he returned.

During those two weeks, I daydreamed and fantasized about what our next "magical evening" would be like. It seemed that everywhere I turned I saw or heard the words "Paris," "France," and "French." Certain that these were "signs" from the Universe, I assumed that Claude was the man I'd waited a lifetime for. On the evening of our dinner, I asked Claude where he had been on his business trip, to which he replied, "In Paris, with my wife." Needless to say, our relationship ended, but it did inspire me to work at honing my skills in "sign" interpretation.

As I pondered what I could learn from this experience, I realized that I had interpreted these signs more from my mind than from my heart. In reality, I gave the Paris messages the meaning I wanted them to have. Afraid that Claude might not be "the right man," I strove to avoid hearing any inner messages to the contrary. In all honesty, I often felt uneasy and tried to convince myself of the validity of my interpretation. In essence, the "knowing" was not complete but fragmented, with snippets of fear and anxiety lurking beneath the surface.

As with the many false voices masquerading as intuition, what we think of as synchronicity may be nothing more than a creation of our mind. For example, when we are obsessed with something or want something very badly, we may invent signs that aren't really there. We may also read the signs incorrectly, as I did with the wayward Frenchman. Since that time, I have learned to distinguish between what I want and what I know. The knowing that accompanies a real synchronicitous experience originates in the heart and resonates throughout every part of the being. In these cases, fear and doubt are virtually nonexistent. All that remains is a quiet, complete knowing that requires no explanations, no defenses, and no rationalizations.

Synchronicity, like intuition, needs observation and practice to master. And the more we recognize it and interpret it correctly, the more it occurs, bringing the magic of another dimension into our lives.

All of us have synchronistic experiences daily, although we usually are unaware of them. To this I say, stop, look, and listen, but be discerning. Recognize that one's mind can turn anything into a sign and can also misinterpret the messages. But with that caveat, let me encourage you to be open to the synchronicity all around us. The book you are compelled to take down from the shelf just might contain some information to help you, or even transform your life. That's what happened to me with Emerson: a desperate moment, a book that seemed to call to me, and then . . . some lifesaving wisdom that ultimately helped me create a new life.

Be receptive to the synchronicities of your own life. They may come in the form of a book, a word, a person, or an event. Yet, because of their connection with the whole, they can offer us insights that can heal, as well as inspire. Like intuition, synchronicities are God's messengers, and they have something to tell you, if you open your ears and listen to your heart.

Revelation

> We distinguish the announcements of the soul, its manifestations of its own nature, by the term Revelation. These are always attended by the emotion of the sublime.
> —"The Over-Soul"

Revelations are also part of the miraculous communication system designed to bring us closer to the God within us. Somewhat different from intuition, revelations fill our beings with what Emerson calls "the emotion of the sublime." In this transcendent state, we can determine truths, both individual and universal, and tap into the energy that will help us integrate these truths into our lives.

Most of us have felt the almost mystical touch of a revelation wash over us. This experience can happen at any time, although it usually occurs when least expected. During these moments, we sense the presence of Divine Intelligence and know that we have come face to face with truth. This truth could be anything from an insight into the nature of God to the solution to a problem. Although revelations usually come in the form of words, the impression left on you goes beyond words, and even beyond the senses.

Saints and mystics have traditionally been the receptors of revelations throughout the ages. One of the best known of these is Joan of Arc, whose divine revelations lifted her out of the realm of the ordinary and into the realm of hero and saint. When we think of Joan and others like her we can hardly imagine ourselves as the recipient of such divine grace. yet in reality, we are not so different from her. For the only difference between mystics and the rest of us is that they have learned, either consciously or unconsciously, how to tap into the divine channel. Accessing this divine channel is always a challenge, because we all need to find our own way to "open it up." Some of us stumble upon it, while the rest of us continue searching. The only direction needed to connect with Infinite Intelligence, however, and the only direction possible, lies in the command "Look within."

Revelations also come in the form of prophecies, which allow us to glimpse the future. For example, after I finished this book, I spent a few tortured months dealing with rejections and negative comments from publishers. Then, on one of the gloomiest days in March, an old friend of mine, who is also a psychic, telephoned me from "out of the blue." Although we hadn't spoken in years, she said I had been in her thoughts lately. After telling her about the rejection of my book, she stated, "You will sell the book on July twenty-fifth." I didn't take her seriously, but the date stuck in my mind, since it was my niece's—and godchild's—birthday. As the summer approached, I forgot all about the psychic prediction and actually gave up on my book, at least that version of it. I was working on a second draft when fate surprised me with the sale of the book—on July twenty-fifth just as my friend had predicted.

Although her "psychic flash" proved accurate and valuable, Emerson cautions us against relying on psychics and the like. His warning alerts us to the dangers of looking to outside authorities for answers, rather than to ourselves. For although psychics are appropriate resources at times, depending on them for answers often prevents us from looking within, thereby diminishing our self-reliance. Instead, we need to cultivate our own revelatory abilities with the knowledge that when the time is right, the answers will appear.

Later on in this chapter, I will explain some of the ways we can make ourselves more receptive to these incoming communications from God. In the meantime, let us turn to the topic of inspiration, which is indeed heaven sent.

Inspiration

> I believe that nothing great and lasting can be done except by
> inspiration, by leaning on the secret augury.
>
> —"Inspiration"

Inspiration. Either we have it or we don't. And if we don't, we
long to know just how to get it. For life without inspiration just
doesn't seem worth living. Yet, what is inspiration and where
does it come from? And how can we, the uninspired, tap into its
power and make it our own?

Emerson believed that inspiration originates from the Universal Mind, or Over-Soul, which contains countless ideas awaiting
expression in the world. When an artist is inspired, it is as if he or
she has connected with some element of creation that is waiting
to be born and has become the willing channel for it. When you
read Van Gogh's letters to his brother Theo, for example, you
can see how his paintings emerged from an energy almost
beyond his control. When inspired, Van Gogh couldn't help
working at his painting. In short, he had to, for he had touched
the "secret augury," and had to carry out its plans.

From this perspective, the saying "Nothing is more powerful
than an idea whose time has come" is very true. For ideas, works
of art, societal innovations, and all creative acts, great or small,
emerge from this Over-Soul, which is the soul of all mankind,
and of God. Better known as the collective unconscious, this soul
operates as a repository through which we can connect with an
idea or any creative act, and, through inspiration, bring this to
pass in the world.

When seen in this light, the "great" achievers of history are no
different from you and me. Their gift—that spark that made
their lives grand rather than mediocre—resulted from their
openness to the divine channels. In other words, they were open
and willing vehicles for carrying out some element of creation.

Inspiration is not only the domain of the artist, but is sought
after by creators in all fields, even in the field of parenting. For as

every parent knows, the inspired moments of child-rearing seem to make all the other ones worthwhile. In fact, inspiration can infuse any task with energy and ease of accomplishment. And whether that task is writing a book, developing an invention, raising a child, or creating a loving moment, someone has been charged with the fire of inspiration and is engaged in the creative process.

When inspiration lights our way, we can often see clearly the solution to a problem or can pave the way for the inception of an idea. Books have been written, societies changed, and inventions made in the name of inspiration. Great works of art owe their existence to inspired creators, as do the discoveries of scientists and the ideas born of philosophers.

The difficulty with inspiration is that it seems to come only in flashes. What we all would like to know is whether there are ways in which we can capture inspiration and hold it a little longer in our lives, thereby becoming receptive channels for Universal Intelligence.

The following guidelines may not only assist in harnessing inspiration, but may also help set the stage for other Universal messengers—such as intuition, synchronicity, and revelation—to appear. And when they do, and are efficiently utilized, we will have begun to develop a relationship with the God within, changing our lives forever.

Pray From Your "Wholeness"

> Prayer is the contemplation of the facts of life from the highest point of view. It is the soliloquy of a beholding and jubilant soul . . . As soon as man is one with God, he will not beg.
>
> —"Self-Reliance"

What exactly is prayer? Traditionally, prayer is the process of asking an external God for something we desire. Whether it be a new job, the perfect mate, or the cessation of an illness, we ask and hope we shall receive. Of course, with this type of prayer, sometimes we receive and sometimes we don't. Unfortunately, for most of us, this is the only prayer we know. Emerson, however, conceived of a different type of prayer, one in which union with God would make all other types of prayer obsolete.

When you pray as Emerson directs, you first must enter into a union with the God within before you begin to "state your case." For example, let's say you want to find the perfect job. First, you enter into a meditative state in which you feel at one with the Divine Energy, and *then* you declare what you want, by using affirmations and declarations of God's presence throughout the Universe. This type of prayer, used by those involved with the Religious Science and Unity religions, does not beg. Instead it assumes that when we are at one with God, all that we desire is already ours; we only need to accept it into our lives.

Obviously each of us, at different times, enjoys different levels of union with the Divine, which ultimately determines the power of the prayer. Using this gauge as a barometer, complete union would net the most effective prayer, and complete separation, the least. So before you pray for anything to be brought into your life, try to sense God's presence within you before you affirm, in your own words, what it is you desire. So instead of asking for something to be brought into your life, state with faith that "Because God is all powerful and exists within me as well as within the Universe, I know that I am *now* established in the perfect career (or whatever it is that you desire) that will enrich me and start me on my path to fulfilling my purpose. Amen." Then let it go, knowing that your desire is already a reality and that it is now manifesting in your world.

As powerful as this type of prayer is, Emerson discouraged praying for what he calls a "particular commodity." Strange as this concept seems, Emerson believed that when we become one with God, all desires cease, because all desires are fulfilled. When Jesus advised us to "Seek first the kingdom of God and all else will be added," he spoke of this same truth.

When we pray for something, we acknowledge our lack of that same something. In oneness, however, wholeness exists and lack disappears, as we realize that we already have that which we desire. In *The Wizard of Oz*, the characters already possessed that which they asked of the Wizard. The scarecrow already had a brain, the tin man a heart, the lion his courage, and Dorothy her home, although they did not know it.

During a particularly desperate time in my life, I called upon a spiritual teacher for guidance and direction. "I need money and my career is going nowhere. I must find out how to get these things!" I told her, the fear of poverty holding me in its grasp. Instead of helping me pray for what I desired, she told me to realize my wholeness, and to know that in truth I needed nothing. "Experience your oneness with God," she said, "and you'll understand that you have all you need within yourself."

She further explained that when we pray out of a sense of lack, we deny the abundance of the Universe, and carry this consciousness of lack with us wherever we go. Even if we get what we desire, soon after, another desire surfaces, and the lack returns, and so on, ad infinitum. Now this is not to say that desires are wrong, for we need goals and direction in life. The problem exists with the *feeling* of lack, which often creates desperation within us.

In a recent interview, Dr. Larry Dossey, author of *Healing Words,* related an interesting discovery of his research. While observing the miracles that have surrounded the recent appearances of the Virgin Mary in Medjugorje, located in the former Yugoslavia, he noted that those people who were the *least* desperate had their prayers answered more often. If this is true, then perhaps those who were not desperate sensed the presence of God within themselves, which gave them faith. And faith, it is easy to see, originates from a consciousness of wholeness rather than of a lack.

So while praying, try to touch the wholeness that exists within you. It will bring you closer to God and to the realization that we can have anything we desire, once we realize all exists within ourselves.

Cultivate Solitude

But if he would know what the great God speaketh, he must
'go into his closet and shut the door,' as Jesus said. God will
not make himself manifest to cowards.
                                                    —"The Over-Soul"

In these fast-paced days of rushing and striving, we have precious little time for solitude. Our lives and our selves somehow
get lost in the shuffle until we virtually become estranged from
our inner beings. The things-to-do list gets longer, while our time
alone gets shorter, leaving us drained, empty, and gasping for
air. What we should seek, however, is none other than the rare-
fied air of that divine part of ourselves that lives within the
"closet" of the heart.

When Emerson says that we must go into our closets and shut
the door, he is referring to a meditative state of mind which
opens us up to God's presence within us. Obviously, any of the
various forms of meditation can lead us to this inner sanctuary,
for they are all valuable; yet, meditating on certain phrases and
images can influence our experience and may actually prevent us
from achieving the pure communication we seek.

When I first began meditating, I started by visualizing my idea
of "the perfect life." I sat for twenty minutes every day, creating
magnificent pictures in my mind of lavish homes, loving relationships, and prosperous lifestyles. In one particular meditation, I
saw myself ascending a circular staircase that led to an emerald
castle—shades of *The Wizard of Oz*. To me, this ascension signi-
fied my rising up from the ashes of what had once been my life.
This elaborate production included musical accompaniment, as
well, such as Wagner's *Siegfried Idyll* and Samuel Barber's *Ada-
gio for Strings*. Needless to say, these "meditations" left me in a
state of ecstasy, which I perceived as being filled with God.

As the years went on, however, I gradually understood that
my "pictures" and "ideas" left little room for that still, small
voice to come through. Rather than developing a relationship

with God, I had been programming myself with images that I believed would make me happy. In essence, my solitude included as many diversions as my life did. At this point, I understood that what I needed was to enter into the silence, rather than enter into a preconceived "program." Entering into the silence is a simple, yet profound type of meditation than can bring you closer to the God within.

First of all, you need to find a quiet place and some time during the day. Start by concentrating on your breathing for a few minutes. Really feel your inhalations and exhalations. Then discontinue your concentration on your breathing and let whatever will come into your mind. Allow all extraneous thoughts and fears entry as you try to focus on the deeper thoughts, feelings, messages. While doing this, let your inner self go, as you feel the freedom within. Remember no one or nothing is monitoring you; you needn't control anything. When silence comes, just accept it. When words, feelings, and messages come, accept those too. Deeply accept all—the positive and the negative—that is within you. Embrace the silence as well, knowing that within it is God. Don't try to force a feeling of union with the Divine Energy, but know that if you experience a deeply moving, expansive, and loving energy that frees you, you have touched the eternal.

When I first began this type of meditation, I felt a great deal of fear. Afraid of delving into the silence of my being, I resisted it by either falling asleep or by avoiding it altogether. My constant complaint of "not having enough time," kept me safe from entering into my deepest self, which I feared was filled with dragons. After I sat with and entered completely into my fears, I discovered that they were really just blocked energy that needed to be released and transformed. By facing and feeling them fully, I unblocked the energy, which led me to some of the most rewarding and transforming experiences of my life.

I also discovered that the "horrible things" inside me—anger, sadness, hatred, and fear—were really angels in disguise. Ultimately, they only needed my recognition and acceptance in order to be transformed. Prior to this, I had rejected them, cut them off from myself, so to speak, which left me fragmented, instead of whole. When I finally embraced these "dark" parts, they could be integrated into my being, and could provide me with much-needed energy and creativity.

Most of what I uncovered within, however, was full of such beauty that it inspired me toward reverence. For hidden had been such depths of compassion and love I was almost over-whelmed. I wonder if perhaps we fear this side of ourselves as well, which, like our "dark" side, waits for us within the silence.

I believe that much of our fast-paced, noise-polluted lifestyles originate from our fear of this silence. When people talk about their "fear of being alone," they are really speaking about their deeper fear of silent, uninterrupted solitude. For within this soli-tude, we come face to face with our aloneness, which is terrify-ing. If we persist and go deeper within ourselves, we will find that we are not alone, but that the Infinite is within us. Until we realize this truth, we will run from ourselves and ultimately run from God. Yet, ironically this is what we are really seeking, and never seem to find. When Dorothy in *The Wizard of Oz* talks about finding happiness in her own back yard, and says "There's no place like home," she is, allegorically, speaking about our "real" home that lies within us.

We can run from relationship to relationship, from job to job, from place to place, and from success to success, and still be left wanting. "There must be something more," we say, and never realize that, like Dorothy, we carry our "home" within us.

Visualizations, guided meditations, and the like, are valuable tools on the spiritual path. But like anything else, we must be careful to use these tools to move us closer to God and not far-ther away.

Get Health

> . . . but I will say, get health. No labour, pains, temperance, poverty, nor exercise, that can gain it, must be grudged. For sickness is a cannibal which eats up all the life and youth it can lay hold of, and absorbs its own sons and daughters.
>
> —"Considerations by the Way"

As I write this section, I am fighting the symptoms of the all-too-common cold. Frustrated and sniffling, I notice that my powers of intuition and revelation are congested, along with my head. My mental clarity is also diminished, as is my energy level. I accomplish significantly less during these ill periods, my writing productivity decreased and other projects postponed. Spiritually speaking, I am aware that my communication with God decreases as well, both in quantity and quality.

Emerson understood how illness inhibits our spiritual growth and eats away at our inner strength. Like many of us, he suffered from various illnesses much of his life, though still struggling to attain the spiritual evolution he wrote so eloquently about. He appreciated the connection between mind, body, psyche, and spirit; and he knew in total health all these work together in harmony.

In recent years, much has been written about the mind/body connection and about how our emotions affect our health. Emerson acknowledged this relationship, but also stressed the opposite, namely that our health affects our emotions.

I know that when I am sick, my outlook suffers. Sometimes I am irritable and unduly pessimistic. At others, I am maudlin and cry at the merest insult. During these times, I hardly have the strength to meditate, let alone the inclination. On the other hand, when my health returns, my view of life improves as well, as my body rejoices in the Divine Energy that seemed absent during my illness.

Of course, we all may know a few inspiring individuals who manage to remain cheerful throughout the worst illnesses. Certain exceptional people even use their illnesses to enhance their spiritual lives and, in so doing, to rise above their affliction. Unfortunately most of us, while sick, operate at lower levels of efficiency in all areas: physically, emotionally, spiritually, and psychically.

One way to increase the efficiency and health of all the various aspects of ourselves is to live from truth, rather than appearances. Our health suffers when, out of fear and insecurity, we deny our feelings and thoughts. When we choose to work at a career that does not resonate with our inner being, our health deteriorates, though often in such subtle ways that we do not notice it until, faced with a serious illness, we look back and see how self-denial and repression wore away at the immune system.

In the past decade, the medical community has finally recognized how diet, along with psychological health, contributes to the breakdown of the immune system. The recent interest in environmental and food allergies, as well as in the many illnesses caused by a weakened immune system, is opening up a new area in health care that could very well revolutionize medicine as we know it. An increasing number of alternative physicians have been able to heal people just by changing their diets and altering their environments. The population of the developed world has consumed sugar-laden, chemically processed foods for decades now. Our homes—our bodies, as well—have been cleaned and sprayed with dangerous products that diminish our natural immunity, thereby leaving us open to illnesses.

Often when the immune system weakens, one develops allergies, which compound the problem. As long as we continue to eat or expose ourselves to the allergenic substance, our immunity decreases even more, greatly increasing our chances of contracting a serious disease. The allergies I am talking about don't necessarily appear in the usual ways, such as hives and sneezing; instead they show themselves in more subtle symptoms, such as weight gain, depression, headaches, and constipation.

I have known people who have virtually changed their lives after discovering an allergy to wheat. Their minds cleared, their energy returned, and their zest for life was renewed just by an alteration in diet. I've also seen migraine headaches cured by removing all perfumes from a person's environment, and depressions have been known to disappear when an allergenic food or substance is removed from a sufferer's life.

The increasing use of alternative and holistic medicine is helping many of us to develop an optimal level of health. At the same time, the recent movement toward recovery and spiritual evolution is leading us toward a degree of fulfillment and happiness rarely known before. As we rid our emotional lives of imbalances, our bodies, like our spiritual and psychic aspects, also need cleansing and purification. As the years go by, I am aware that the healthier I become emotionally, the more my body requires an equally healthy style of living. Gradually, as I healed emotionally, my body reacted to toxic and unhealthy substances, seeming to reject unhealthy foods, such as sugar, caffeine, and alcohol, by developing allergies to them.

Before you start any self-help program, I strongly recommend a visit to an alternative health practitioner—many of them are medical doctors as well—so he or she can help determine how many of your problems stem from nutritional deficiencies, a weakened immune system, or an allergy. Oftentimes, the right nutritional program or diagnosis of an allergy can alleviate chronic depression more efficiently and quickly than psychotherapy.

In addition, your intuition—especially when developed—can help you discern exactly what your body needs and wants. For example, if your inner voice keeps telling you to exercise, follow it. Remember, though, this inner voice doesn't contain any of the "shoulds" we are all too familiar with. Commands that you *should* exercise three times a week are useless unless your intuition is doing the speaking. For when your intuition is guiding you, you can be sure that your body will accept its directives with ease, rather than resistance.

In Shakti Gawain's book, *Living in the Light,* she suggests using our intuition to determine our diets. She advises us to listen to what foods our bodies want, and then to eat them. For those of us who fear we would gorge ourselves on chocolate sundaes, she explains that our bodies may desire unhealthy foods at first, but that eventually our intuition will lead us to eat the best foods for our individual needs. A word of caution, however: be aware that we often crave foods to which we are allergic. Alternative health professionals know this and suggest that all allergenic foods must be eliminated from the diet before the intuition can kick in.

Holistic medicine asks us to examine all the aspects and details of our lives through the lens of total self-recovery. We can no longer fragment our health care by dealing only with the body or with the mind. The mind, body, spirit, and psyche are bound together individually as well as globally. When we honor and

care for all parts of our being, as we do the world, we open ourselves up to greater dimensions of living than ever before.

Spend Time With Nature

> Certain localities, as mountain-tops, the seaside, the shores
> of rivers and rapid brooks, natural parks of oak and pine,
> where the ground is smooth and unencumbered, are exci-
> tants of the muse.
>
> —"Inspiration"

In Somerset Maugham's novel *The Razor's Edge*, Larry Dar-
rell embarks upon a search for Universal Truth. His journey
takes him to many places, and although he obtains knowledge
along the way, he is still left wanting. In India, however, a spiritual teacher advises him to go up into the mountains, suggesting
that many strange and wonderful things happen there. Darrel
follows the teacher's advice, and finally achieves his goal while
meditating on the proverbial mountaintop. For it is here he dis-
covers that he and God are one.

It is not an accident that Maugham chose a mountaintop for
his protagonist's place of transformation. Spiritual seekers
throughout history have scaled the heights of many peaks, hoping to achieve the oneness and bliss we are all seeking. Emerson
knew the magical quality of nature, and encouraged his readers
to spend as much time as they could in this divine realm. For
here, he believed, lay hidden the secrets of the Universe. By observing and communing with nature, Emerson opened himself
up to many insights and revelations. He believed that everything
in nature pointed to a corresponding spiritual truth, and that one
could sense the unity of "all that is" within these outdoor ha-
vens. For instance, he writes "when the fruit is ripe, it falls," an
observation both of a natural occurrence and of the mystery of
timing in our lives. The natural ripening and falling of the fruit
tells him that things happen when they—or we—are ready, and
not before.

Believing God to be inherent in nature, Emerson questioned

the traditional Christian theologies which often viewed nature and the human body as evil and dark as opposed to the soul and spirit which were light. Even the Christian devil had taken on the image of the European nature god, Pan, thereby representing nature as evil. Emerson, however, sensed the divine emanating from each tree, brook, and ocean.

By spending time in nature, each of us can connect with this Divine Energy and absorb its wisdom. For instance, a walk in the woods may work wonders when you are devoid of inspiration and spiritual energy. By listening quietly to the rustling of the leaves, you might be revitalized, energized. Often when rejuvenated, you will find yourself full of childlike wonder, your faith reborn while you breathe in the air and take in the sights. Your heart may open at the sight of deer running by, leaving you primed and ready for those inner communications you long to initiate.

Emerson stated that while in nature he felt nothing harmful could happen to him, and he wrote of nature's ability to lessen even the greatest sorrow. Some time ago, when nothing seemed to be going well in my life, I walked in the woods every day. As the warm rush of air brought hope to my heart, I'd notice my sorrow evaporating. During these moments, I'd feel blissfully happy, as I realized that all I needed was right there in those woods. Strangely whole and content, even in the midst of unhappiness, I knew that a healing was taking place and that it had nothing to do with any change in circumstances. Many times, while walking, a feeling of oneness washed over me, helping me to see the potential for growth inherent in my situation.

Ideas for articles and other writing projects have come to me while in nature. It is as if the woods and I are communicating on a deep level, which makes me receptive to the ideas that seem to fall gently, like leaves, into my waiting mind. For in these natural settings, we can let go of our social roles and worldly burdens and come away refreshed, with a new outlook on life. When people want to "recharge their batteries," they often head for the country, the seashore, or the mountains. Instinctively, we know of nature's power to heal, inspire, and transform. What we need to do is not wait until we are exhausted and spent, but turn to nature daily, if we can, and drink from its inexhaustible springs.

Engage in Meaningful Conversations

> Conversation, which, when it is best, is a series of intoxications.
>
> —"Inspiration"

Most of our conversations concern themselves with such meaningless subjects that we come away from them drained and uninspired. Topics such as the weather, the price of milk, or what happened on our favorite television show last night have their place, but they are often all we talk about. Concerned with safety and maintaining the status quo, our ego only allows so-called safe subjects into our communications. Afraid of opening a "pandora's box," it guards us against subjects with any depth and intimacy. Family relationships seem especially prone to this "guarding," because of long-established roles and heavily entrenched patterns.

In many of our families, we have difficulty communicating in meaningful and intimate ways. We'd rather engage in meaningless chatter than actually tell a family member our deepest thoughts and feelings. After a while, this pattern becomes established, almost part of a relationship contract. John Bradshaw often talks about the "no talk, no feel," rule operating in many families, which he believes creates a barrier to intimacy. These barriers can resemble brick walls, and require much time and effort to penetrate. Sometimes, when they cannot be penetrated, we just have to "let them be."

Your intuition can provide you with the guidance you seek when facing intimacy barriers. For example, in my own family, I have a sense of the person I can open up to, and the one I can't. Sometimes, of course, that sense misdirects me and I end up banging on a brick wall, but most of the time its guidance is unerring. I have learned not to waste my energy on those family relationships that hide behind impenetrable walls, but instead to spend my time on the ones with an opening or two.

Emerson characterized some family gatherings as nothing more than a room full of strangers. For when affinity is lacking, and the barriers are well-forged, spending time with one's family provides no real intimacy or conversation.

Emerson also noted that when two people communicate deeply, an invisible third party enters, resulting from the combination of the two. This "third party"—Emerson sometimes refers to it as God—adds another dimension to the conversation, often sparking revelations and fine-tuning intuition. Not limited to only two people, this phenomenon occurs in every worthwhile conversation, whether the group be large or small.

Oftentimes, this "group mind" gets ignited and inspires one or more of the members, creatively or with the solution to a problem. Many of my own "revelations" emerge out of inspired and energized conversation. When engaging in this type of communication, I expand and am oblivious to any boundary, be it physical, intellectual, or spiritual. Ideas seem to flow unimpeded through my mind, which then is in harmony with my heart and spirit, thus fueling these new thoughts.

As Emerson observed, some ideas originate from our communications with ourselves, or with the God within; others take two or more of us to find. For in inspired conversation, ideas hover about and within us, awaiting discovery. By participating in soulful discussion, we magnetize these ideas toward us, then call them our own.

Whenever I finish one of these stimulating conversations, I walk away inspired and ready for universal wisdom to come through. Usually my head is clear, and I am ready for action. And most of the time, the action required has to do with the idea implanted in my mind. Inventions and new ways of living come to us during or after meaningful conversations, because two or more minds magnetized one another.

Although I realize that we all need to talk about the weather from time to time, a steady diet of that kind of talk will result in malnutrition of the soul. Slowly, through superficial conversation or malicious gossip, we will starve ourselves of the energy of the Universe. So open up, explore ideas with others, ask your family members how they feel about them, and see what happens. Not everyone will be receptive, but you will discover those with whom vital conversations can be pursued. And when your circle is enlarged, you too will be enlarged by conversations which expand and elevate your consciousness.

Obstructing the Channels

> The lesson is forcibly taught by these observations, that our life might be much easier and simpler than we make it; that the world might be a happier place than it is; that there is no need of struggles, convulsions, and despairs.
> —"Spiritual Laws"

Even though we are equipped with a direct line to a higher power, most of us never make full use of this potential. Either we refuse to acknowledge the gift, or else we never quite take the steps needed to solidify this inner relationship. Perhaps our lives are too busy for us to get away and spend some time alone. Or maybe we are just too lazy and frightened to break the patterns that keep us from living as we want to live.

Emerson believed that God provides us with the ways and means to achieve a happy and fulfilled life. By discovering our inner voice and following its directions, we can make the choices and decisions that will enable us to fulfill our potential. And by observing life and nature, we can understand the Universal laws and live in harmony with them. Why then, if all this is possible, do we ignore our intuition, deny our synchronicities, and close ourselves off from revelation and inspiration?

Consider what we learn as babies. We are completely dependent upon external sources for sustenance and emotional fulfillment; along with the usual physical expressions of love, we are given toys to entertain us, blankets to comfort us, and food to nourish us. As we grow older, however, an increasing self-reliance should ensure, slowly weaning us away from dependency on our family. Unfortunately, the opposite often occurs.

Instead of developing our inner being, we complicate the dependency. We now need approbation and good grades in order to feel successful, the acceptance of our peers in order to feel good about ourselves. And we continue to need approval from our family in order to feel ourselves worthy of the best life has to offer. In essence, our programming ensures that we continue to look without for our happiness, rather than within.

And the world distracts us from our inner life. Television, movies, video games, clothes, homes, and various other consumables and forms of entertainment draw our attention away from ourselves and toward the glittering and noisy distractions around us. It's no wonder that many of us lead spiritually malnourished and emotionally dysfunctional lives.

Yet, in spite of all this "programming" in the wrong direction, we can learn how to look to the God within for love and fulfillment. And we must, for if we don't find them there, we'll never find them anywhere. External glories may satisfy us for a while, yet our emptiness will always return, goading us onward until we, by accident or by design, stumble upon the real treasure that lies within. And that will never be found in a new Jaguar or in a lover's eyes, which brings me to another reason we continually reject our divine birthright.

As children, we learn that if we do right, acceptance follows, and if we do wrong, rejection results. Acceptance, of course, feels good, while rejection feels bad. So life becomes nothing more than a desperate search for acceptance, with our fear of rejection driving us. To gain acceptance, we may do anything from saying things we don't mean to living in the "right" neighborhood and having the "right" friends. What is more unfortunate, however, is that we sometimes run from that which will benefit us the most, just to be accepted.

Remember the time you got the only A in the class? Or the time you won the award? What happened? Think back now. Didn't you feel different and separate from your peers? Did they reject you out of jealousy or just because you weren't "one of them" anymore? How did it feel? At that moment, wouldn't you have done anything to feel like "one of the group" again?

If you're like most of us, you'll do anything to "fit in" with the particular group to which you belong. Whether you have to take a drink, support the right political party, or walk on coals, you'll do it so rejection won't inflict more wounds upon your already battered heart. On a larger scale, you might even deny yourself access to the God within, just so you won't have to experience that feeling of alienation from your friends, your family, and perhaps even your society.

Try to remember a time when everything was going well for you in your life. Naturally, you shared your joy with friends and family, who hopefully supported you. And in many cases, they *do* support you, especially if your accomplishments fit in with their agenda. But what if they don't? What if they just sit in silence or change the subject? Or what if they make some self-pitying remark? Do their reactions make you feel guilty for being happy?

Oftentimes, on subtle levels, we sense that if we get ahead, others will reject us. Family members may resent our success. Or we might not have anything in common anymore with our particular group. This fear of rejection also applies to our spiritual growth. We fear that if we truly utilize and activate our spiritual center and live from that, rather than from outside cues, we will move a bit out of the ring of normal human experience. We instinctively fear that if we "open up" and develop this relationship within ourselves, our lives will change, as will some of the people in them. And this fear prevents us from fully developing our spiritual potential—or any other potential for that matter.

The fear, is, on some levels, a valid one, for as we move ahead spiritually and learn to relate to the God within, we will feel somewhat apart from the crowd. Yet, if we continue on this path, we will find that the unity and oneness that eventually result will connect us with our fellow humans on deeper levels. Although we may no longer be partners in misery and mediocrity, we will become joined by that part of us that exists within all beings and within all things. When this happens, we will no longer need acceptance, for separateness will not exist. Then, and only then, will we be fed from the eternal spring within, instead of the temporal world without.

The truth is, we cannot help each other by staying "stuck" in negative patterns or by not living up to our fullest potential. In the long run, other people will be helped by our example, by our showing them that they too can find fulfillment and happiness, that they too can know spiritual ecstasy, and that they too can become spiritual beings who enjoy a relationship with their inner selves. It's up to us. The old game of acceptance and rejection has brought us nothing but mediocrity and futility. The new game of self-discovery and self-acceptance can bring us everything.

· 3 ·

The Third Secret
Understand the Law of Compensation

If this doctrine could be stated in terms with any resemblance
to those bright intuitions in which this truth is sometimes
revealed to us, it would be a star in many dark hours and
crooked passages in our journey that would not suffer us to
lose our way.

—"Compensation"

At times, the world seems horribly unfair and chaotic, completely devoid of any justice. We work hard, follow all the
"rules," yet still find it difficult to survive. We wonder why, just
as soon as everything comes together in someone's life, he develops a life-threatening illness. Or why someone else has to suffer
the loss of a child. When we ourselves experience tragedy or re-
versal, we long to shake our fists at Fate and bellow, "Why me?"

What if I told you that a Universal law exists that compensates
us for all our hardships and failings? And that hidden within
each negative circumstance lies an equally positive potential,
waiting to be accepted and implemented in our lives. Would it
surprise you to know that every crime is punished and that every
good action is rewarded? And that every gain we make includes
a loss on some level, every loss a gain?

All these scenarios, along with others, are part of the law of
compensation, which Emerson perceived as the balancing force
within the Universe. No one escapes from the effects of this law,
which operates like the scales of justice. Because of this law, we
reap what we sow, even though the payment may not come in
the form we expect.

I've often heard people complain that they've given so much to such and such a cause or person, and never been repaid or appreciated for their efforts. Like a horse with blinders, they only look in one direction for their payment, and usually it is where they feel they "gave" so unselfishly. Did they ever stop to think that their payment may come to them in another way? That time you showed compassion to an unappreciative friend may be repaid by the love of a child. Or the care you squandered on a dead-end relationship may return to you through friends, employers, or in a thousand other ways. In other words, we need a clearer and more expanded vision to understand how the law of compensation operates in our lives.

In order to observe this immutable law in operation, we sometimes need to look beneath the surfaces of things, people, and events. We need to examine the criminal's heart and soul, to determine where the real punishment is levied. We need to see beyond the tragic circumstance to the gift that lies waiting. And we need to peer behind every facade of success, knowing that appearances often lie and that a person's soul tells the real story.

This view of life may seem like rationalization to some, and rather Pollyannaish to others. But life has taught me, by observation and experience, that the law of compensation does indeed exist and that it operates within our lives, mostly without our knowledge, though a working knowledge of this law and its facets is invaluable, for that will assist you in making the most of your life, and of yourself. Through your intuition, it will guide and enlighten you regarding hidden meanings and unrecognized gifts. It may also let you know when you've overstepped the bounds and may keep many so-called accidents and tragedies at bay. In essence, the law of compensation will be, as Emerson called it, a "star" that leads us toward good, keeps us from harm, and, most importantly, helps us not to lose our way.

Find the Gift in Every Tragedy

> The changes which break up at short intervals the prosperity
> of men are advertisements of a nature whose law is growth.

> Every soul is by this intrinsic necessity quitting its whole system of things, its friends, and home, and laws, and faith, as the shellfish crawls out of its beautiful but stony case, because it no longer admits of its growth, and slowly forms a new house.
>
> —"Compensation"

When my life fell apart in 1987, I thought I had the curse of the century upon me. My husband's business failed along with the 1980s, leaving him a million dollars in debt. To add to this little drama, he ran off with another woman, leaving me without any means of support. We lost our four-hundred-thousand-dollar home to the bank, and sold our furniture to pay the bills. My car was repossessed, my money was gone, and my future looked bleak.

With nowhere else to go, I moved back to my mother's house, toting a wardrobe that belied my poverty. "At least they can't take your clothes, Mare," my attorney once said, as he perfunctorily paid himself with the little money I had left. "Well, that's what you get for living such a high life." And he was right. I had lived high, and foolishly hadn't prepared to support myself. Yes, I had a master's degree in English Literature, but how could I use it, what could I do?

During these dark days, I pitied myself constantly and incessantly wondered Why me? Until Emerson's essay "Compensation" answered my questions and altered my life.

In it, he teaches us that tragedy comes to us with a message, encouraging us to change and to grow in a new and perhaps different direction. In other words, tragedies are nature's warnings that alert us when something is wrong with the way we are living. Sometimes we need a small change, and sometimes we need a complete overhaul. In my case, nothing less than major surgery was required. I had to look at myself and at my life with glaring honesty to see if I could determine what the Universe wanted me to do.

So at thirty-two, I began a new path; one that would ultimately lead me toward myself, rather than away. And one that would eventually bring me more joy and fulfillment than I ever imagined. Looking back on that time, I thank God that my house of cards came tumbling down, for it gave me the chance to examine my life and to change it in countless positive ways. Now I can honestly say that the worst tragedy of my life ultimately provided the key to the greatest realizations of my life.

One of the most important of these was that nature operates in a constant state of flux. In order to move with the harmony of the Universe, we must grow and change daily. Evolution didn't stop with the Neanderthal. It occurs every day, within every one of us. However, most of us resist this change, which blocks the flow of energy within us and creates disturbances, problems, and tragedies both within our hearts and in the circumstances of our lives. What these difficulties provide us with, however, are opportunities to evolve to a new level. If we "get the message," and make the change, we needn't repeat the episode again. Unfortunately, most of us don't discover the purpose, so we repeat the same negative situation over and over, creating patterns that are hard to break.

More than a run of "bad luck," patterns that repeat themselves are nothing more than promptings from our inner self, encouraging us to change. Perhaps all we need to do is change our diet or the type of person we date or the way we spend our free time. It may be a new philosophy of life is called for, perhaps a new relationship with the Universe. The list is endless, but the message is the same: we need to grow.

When we see someone go through one painful relationship after another, we have to wonder why. Unfortunately, many women—and men—feel that they *must* have a relationship to survive. This belief does nothing but create a pattern of one unsatisfactory involvement after another.

Once a person realizes that he or she is whole, and not a fragment looking for another broken piece, a healthy relationship can finally be created, founded not on neediness but on wholeness. And with wholeness comes choice. Dependent relationships have nothing to do with choice, for they compel us by their very nature—dependency.

It took me many painful relationships to get to this point, but when I did, I found the man of my dreams. Before that happened,

I needed to feel that I was OK alone, that I could happily live my life that way. Not coincidentally, the man I attracted also felt whole and complete without a woman! I've often told friends this is the first healthy relationship I've had. But believe me, I wouldn't be where I am now if I had ignored nature's gentle—and sometimes not so gentle—nudgings toward discovering my wholeness.

Looking back, I can clearly see how financial and personal hardship spurred me on toward wholeness and success. Other situations may require a more discerning eye to perceive and reap the benefits. The truth is, however, all negative situations can be used to help us evolve spiritually, emotionally, physically, creatively, and intellectually.

For example, perhaps you've been saddled with poor health much of your life. Unfair, you think, because you've missed out on many of life's pleasures. But let's take a moment to reflect on what could have been gained from this situation, if only you'd unlocked the treasure chest. Perhaps, because of your infirmity, you could have read many books and really developed your mind. Or you could have taken up painting, or some other form of art, and discovered you have real talent. Charles Darwin once said that he never would have accomplished so much if he hadn't been such an invalid. Elizabeth Barrett Browning wrote lovely poetry while in her sickbed, and brightened the world from her little corner.

Emerson himself dealt with sickness, death, and disappointment all his life, yet always chose to grow from his tragedies, rather than wither. All of us can do the same, for by learning and growing from our disappointments, we can achieve life's greatest purpose: the healing and evolution of our soul.

Don't Run From Negativity

And we are now men, and must accept in the highest mind
the same transcendent destiny, and not minors and invalids
in a protected corner, not cowards fleeing before a revolu-

tion, but guides, redeemers, and benefactors, obeying the
Almighty effort and advancing on Chaos and the Dark.

—"Self-Reliance"

Throughout the years, meaningful phrases have helped to inspire me and to guide me through life's more challenging moments. One such line from *The Snows of Kilimanjaro,* comes to
mind whenever I want to avoid, or run away from, something
unpleasant. I can still hear that line clearly, although I haven't
seen the movie for some time: "It's when you run away that
you're most likely to stumble and fall." Yet run away we do,
from our problems, our world, and even from our thoughts.

The recent movement toward spiritual evolution and self-
recovery has spawned wonderful new ways of dealing with life
and its many challenges. Many self-help and "New Age" ideas
have been promulgated through books, workshops, and lectures.
These can provide help in our transformation. Through these
avenues, many people have been inspired to change their negative life patterns into positive ones. One of the potential problem
areas within this "new" philosophy, however, is its populariza-
tion of avoiding or controlling negative thoughts. Originally
conceived as positive thinking, this type of program, though po-
tentially helpful, can become just another means of running
away.

When I first developed an interest in self-help and new age
studies, I fell in line with this program of avoiding all negative
thoughts. Constantly on guard, I worried my way through my
days, afraid that some negative thinking would pop up and ruin
my life. Steeped in the concept "Your thoughts create your reality," I lived in fear of my own mind, hoping that I could control
my life by allowing only positive thoughts entry.

After a while, I discovered the futility of this exercise. For no
matter how hard I tried, uncontrollable things happened, even
though I stood watch over my mind. As a matter of fact, living
this way drained me of energy and created some unnecessary
guilt. Because I believed my thoughts created my reality, I
blamed myself for every "negative" event in my life. "Must have

let a negative thought in," I surmised, as I berated myself for my supposed weakness.

Then one day I realized that what I was really doing was running away from my thoughts, in the same way I used to run away from the problems in my life. After this realization, and after some reading on the subject, I understood that anything repressed or denied does not disappear. Instead, it buries itself in the subconscious, and usually surfaces in more destructive ways later on. By not dealing with my own negativity, I created a backlog that was sure to explode one day, leaving me with more problems than if I had just let those thoughts be.

Rather than specific thoughts creating our reality, I believe it is our level of consciousness that possesses *some* power to alter our reality. Beyond that, who among us really knows and understands all the reasons why our lives are as they are?

Although Emerson encouraged optimism and faith, he also understood that running from the dark side of life would only intensify and empower it. When he talks about "advancing on Chaos and the Dark," he inspires us to meet these demons head on, rather than retreat in fear. For example, let's say that when a relationship ends, you feel excruciating pain inside. I'm not talking about natural grief, but about any overly intense feelings of desolation, unworthiness, and despair. Rather than dulling this pain with your usual diversions, you would do better to allow yourself to feel the pain completely.

There are some very specific techniques you can use to do that, called "breath work." Emotional pain may actually manifest as physical pain, such as a strained sensation in the area of the heart. When we "breathe into" these painful areas, we actually direct our breath to the aching area and deeply inhale and exhale into the pain. Often this surface pain indicates a deeper wound within—perhaps from some previous trauma—that needs attention and healing. (You may experience nausea along with the pain.) If so, breathing will uncover that wound so that it can be dealt with directly, by whatever means you feel is best. Sometimes therapy is a necessary adjunct to breath work, but many times just the breathing process itself is all we need to feel our pain completely, so that we can release it.

When I sit and breathe into my pain, allowing it "to be," I almost always experience a healing. For oftentimes, the pain that gets activated by the unhappy experiences of our lives has at its core a deeply wounded part that has been discarded and ignored. This is the "original pain" that John Bradshaw talks about, which originates from childhood. Unfortunately, if we just feel the surface pain, without dealing with the wound beneath it, we will continue to create situations that activate this pain, again and again.

Carl Jung, the Swiss psychiatrist, believed that a natural force exists within our psyches and that it moves us inextricably toward wholeness. In other words, the pain and negative experiences of our lives occur in order to reveal our wounded parts, so that we can heal them. And the only way we can heal them is to accept them and experience them fully.

Most of us are afraid that if we really felt all of our pain and emptiness, we would die. I know I did, when I first began to allow my pain to "come up" instead of pushing it back down. I recall one night when, after facing a situation that brought up my fears of abandonment, I meditated and breathed into one of these deeply painful pockets. Knowing that this pain was out of proportion to the present situation, I committed myself to getting to the core of it by sitting and feeling it completely. At first, the pain seemed almost unbearable, but I continued, determined to heal this old wound. After a few minutes, I felt a lightness in my chest. In a few more moments, I experienced an unbelievable sense of energy and freedom. As I continued, I noticed my heart opening as I became aware of surges of love and compassion for myself and for all the world. At this point, I knew that my wound had finally been embraced and healed.

Because of that experience, I now look at pain as a beacon to light my way toward a new level of healing and wholeness. Sometimes I can heal a wound in one sitting, sometimes it takes many, but always it requires acceptance, both of the wound and of myself. This technique works equally well with negative beliefs and with fears, that may be inhibiting you. The bottom line is, by running from them, you empower them to contaminate your life; whereas by moving into them, you move beyond them.

By facing your negativity, I don't mean to suggest wallowing in it or obsessing about it. For a consistent negative attitude can and will affect your life in less than positive ways. What I do mean is, see the negativity—whatever it may be—accept it— without fear—and move into it, not away from it. In this way, you dispel its power and empower yourself. Then, and only then, will you be able to develop a truly positive attitude, one based on strength, love, and healing, rather than on fear.

Transform Your Faults

> The good are befriended even by weakness and defect. As no man had ever a point of pride that was not injurious to him, so no man had ever a defect that was not somewhere made useful to him. Every man in his lifetime needs to thank his faults. Our strength grows out of our weakness.
>
> —"Compensation"

Almost everyone spends a lifetime striving for perfection. We futilely seek the perfect body, the perfect relationship, the perfect job, and the perfect home, while longing to become perfect our- selves. While caught up in this "search," our faults and weak- nesses often become abhorrent to us, leading us far away from the self-love we so desperately need for fulfillment.

Lucille Ball once said, "Love yourself first and everything else falls into line." This first lady of comedy understood, like many before and after her, the transforming power of self-love. But what about our faults? Are we to love them too, or are we to despise and eradicate them in any way we can?

Emerson understood that we must accept and love our faults and weaknesses, as well as our attributes and strengths. For without this total self-acceptance, we remain fragmented. In other words, if we accept only our good qualities, and reject our bad, we are in a very real sense rejecting part of ourselves. As long as we do, we prevent ourselves from ever experiencing the healing power of self-love.

Most of my life, I lived with this kind of self-rejection, hating certain aspects of myself. For instance, I hated my feelings of inadequacy and insecurity, and tried to bury them underneath a blanket of contrived sophistication and overconfidence. Instead of curing this supposed "weak link" in my chain of being, my efforts to bury it only intensified those feelings, forcing me to redouble my efforts to conceal them. I often turned to alcohol to help cover up the insecurity I so desperately fought to hide. Other coverups—clothes, possessions, men, and money—also provided me with a facade of self-confidence.

Many other aspects of myself were fair game for this crippling self-rejection. My self-esteem remained low while I persisted in hating my "faults" and trying to push them away. After years of futilely trying to rid myself of faults that always seemed to reappear, I finally learned that they would never lose their power to hurt me until I accepted and loved them. Inspired by Carl Jung's idea on the importance of accepting all parts of ourselves, I quickly saw the faults that I had struggled with for years lose their negative charge. When that happens, they can be integrated into our being, and we can move toward the wholeness that only self-love can bring.

Emerson understood that we could not reach our full potential until we accepted our faults. He also realized, like Jung, that without acceptance no real change is possible. Though we may temporarily hide our faults, they will never go away.

A few years ago, I asked a Zen meditation teacher his advice regarding a certain "character flaw," which had caused me difficulties for many years. Sensing my disdain of this flaw, he replied, "First you must accept this seeming fault; then you must be aware of when it comes up. That is all. Nature will take care of the rest."

Surprised, I thought long and hard about the teacher's advice, until I understood that as long as I hated this part of myself, it would continue to torment me. I also realized that perhaps I had been trying too hard to change, and I transformed my zealousness into a quiet inner commitment. Peace then overtook me, as I finally accepted myself, flaws and all. This shift of perspective, which included a heightened awareness, an inner commitment, and a loving acceptance, led me toward transformation.

Obviously, certain faults are more damaging than others, and require immediate attention. Faults such as alcoholism or violent rage, for example, need transformation more than less damaging ones, such as laziness or shyness. Even in these difficult cases, acceptance is still the rule, for rejection will only make the problem worse. Like any weakness, we need to accept serious faults as part of our being and try to understand them. After the initial act of acceptance, professional help may be needed, especially for more difficult problems. However, it is essential to find a therapist or support group that will not fragment us more by encouraging rejection of our faults.

In the case of less serious faults, try the Jungian technique of "active imagination," in which you personify the particular fault, converse with it, and find out what it wants. For example, let's say that you gossip habitually and want to stop doing so. During a meditation, let the gossiping part show itself to you—in any visual form—and then ask it why it enjoys gossiping. It may respond that it wants to be accepted among certain people, or that it gossips because it wants to avoid talking about intimate things. It may also have a desire to appear better than others by putting other people down.

After you discover the reason, however, you then need to find a way to fulfill its need. For instance, if that gossiping part of you needs acceptance, then you yourself must accept it; after all, self-acceptance has the power to transform, as well as heal. If it wants to appear better than others, perhaps you need to unearth the reason for its feelings of inadequacy. And if it is afraid of intimacy, first seek out the reason for its fears, then gently—with its permission—expose it gradually to more intimate conversational situations.

Obviously, this technique can range from the simple to the complex, in both application and in solution. The important thing, however, is to recognize the part that is causing you trouble, accept it, then develop a relationship with it. Once you realize that your worst faults are often nothing more than the neglected and rejected parts of yourself calling out for acceptance, you will be on your way to healing and transforming them.

Recognizing that our faults may sometimes be blessings can

help us toward accepting and loving them. For instance, our anger may sometimes prevent us from being victimized, while our highly emotional nature may make us more compassionate and caring. Even our neuroses may help us by inspiring us toward a career or toward new discoveries.

I've often heard accomplished musicians say that if they hadn't been so shy, they never would have practiced as much. Oftentimes, an awkwardness with people can be beneficial, if it inspires us toward achievement and self-development. I know that for extended periods of time I felt strange and awkward on dates, so I chose to stay home and read on the weekends, rather than spend time with men who held no interest for me. My intuition told me I needed solitude and I followed it, with great results. For the reading I did helped me develop my career.

During the past few years, I realized that my faults also contributed to the career I am now enjoying. For example, my path of healing and growth helped me uncover my true nature and, consequently, my purpose in life. A less challenging life would probably have led me toward a different, and perhaps less fulfilling, career. Instead, my faults and weaknesses provided the keys to self-realization and self-fulfillment.

If we look at our faults and weaknesses with different eyes and bathe them in the light of acceptance, we will reach our potential with far less effort and in far less time. Any self-improvement program that does not include this type of acceptance is bound to fail, eventually, for as Christ said, "A house divided against itself cannot stand."

Paying the Price

What will you have? quoth God; Pay for it and take it.
—"Compensation"

When I was about eighteen years old, I remember seeing a poster hanging in my best friend's garage that read, "Happy are those who dream dreams and are ready to pay the price to make them come true." During that time in my life, I dreamed great dreams, but thought little about their price. Nevertheless, that statement stayed with me during the next five years, while I searched for my dream of Prince Charming and "happily ever after."

Fortunately for me—or unfortunately, depending on how you look at it—my dreams came true. For after marrying my "prince," my dreams of travel, glamour, excitement, and money began to materialize. Eventually, I was living the life I had imagined as a child and enjoying it immensely. However, certain "friends" and family members informed me that I had not paid the price for my good fortune and I would soon be called upon to balance the books.

After I realized that a price existed and it hadn't been paid, I suddenly felt unworthy and undeserving of my wonderful life, and I waited for the moment when I would be called upon to "pay the piper." After all, I hadn't really suffered much, not in comparison to all the happiness I then enjoyed. Eventually, of course, the bill was presented, and it turned out to be more than I had imagined: suffering, loss, humiliation, and *more* pain. "Well," I thought, as I readied myself for the fall, "this must be what certain people warned me about for years."

Looking back at that time, I now understand that what I thought was a price was really nothing more than my own unworthiness running its self-destructive course. Most of humanity, as I had the pleasure of discovering, believes that we must pay for happiness with equal amounts of sorrow, and so guards itself against too much of a good thing. However, the law of compensation does not demand suffering if you have too much joy or too much love.

Prices do present themselves when we get what we want, but not in the way most of us think. And usually, the price isn't nearly as high as society would like us to believe. What many of us do, unfortunately, is what I did all those years ago. After we reach a goal, and are enjoying the fruits of our labors, we start feeling unworthy and guilty about our good fortune, and start to sabotage it. I've witnessed this scenario many times, in my own life as well as in the the lives of others. Never one to discriminate, self-sabotage affects our careers, relationships, financial success, health, appearance, and any other perceived "gift" of God.

A friend of mine, who had a fulfilling career, a loving marriage, and a beautiful face and body, continually sabotaged other areas of her life. By overspending and making poor financial decisions, she undermined her security, and she sorely neglected her health, so that she suffered from a myriad of ailments. During one of our discussions, she confessed that she had to pay the price for all her blessings by screwing up her health and finances. Talk about self-destruction! At least, my friend was aware of what she was doing. For the majority of us, this process operates rather subconsciously and often continues throughout our lives, convincing us more and more that the price of happiness and success is misery and failure.

All the while, the real price goes unnoticed and therefore unpaid, resulting in more of the same misery that on some level we expect, even desire. To short-circuit this process, we need to rewire our consciousness with the understanding that the law of compensation does not seek to punish or deprive us of our happiness. Instead, the prices that are levied do not harm us, but help us to grow and become more whole.

For instance, the real price of my past successes included enduring the ill will of certain people. When you rise to the top in any area, some people will inevitably be jealous and want you to fail. Others may drop out of your life because they can't deal with your success. One friend of mine, for example, drifted away when I was successful, only to return during my failure with the comment, "I couldn't handle being around all that success. It made me feel too inadequate. Now that you've lost everything, I can be your friend again."

Another price I paid, while successful, was increased visibility. People watched me and my husband more carefully, and some sought our acquaintance for material gain. Salesmen, posing as friends, pressed us to invest in this or that money-making scheme. Others sought an association with our company to enhance their own image.

Before I made the decision to be a writer, I realized that a price would have to be paid for that gift as well. However, this time I knew I didn't have to pay with the coin of suffering, but instead would have to learn to deal with rejection, hard work, and isolation. As much as I love writing, it is sometimes difficult to take the rejection letters, the eternal rewrites, and the hours—sometimes days—of solitude. Yet, because I love my work so much, I am willing to pay the price in order to work at my chosen profession. An added bonus is that when I accept these prices, the "losses" become stepping stones on the path to greater spiritual realization.

You can, of course, perceive any of these "prices" as losses, but I prefer to view them as opportunities for spiritual evolution. For example, when dealing with envious people, we can either become bitter and paranoid or understanding and compassionate. If we choose the latter, our level of consciousness will enable us to love, rather than hate, others. If we lose friends because of success, we can, instead of seething with anger, let them go and bless them on their journey.

When we look at the "prices" paid in our life on our journey to fulfillment, we can accept them with ease and grace—and benefit from them. But most importantly, we need to drop our old programming about paying for our happiness with equal amounts of misery, and then learn to perceive the true price inherent in any goal or achievement. Once we determine that, it can either enhance our spiritual growth or diminish it. As always, the choice is up to us.

Paying your Debts

> It is the part of prudence to face every claimant and pay every just demand on your time, your talents, and your heart. Always pay, for first and last, you must pay your entire debt.
> —"Compensation"

When we think of debts, we usually think of the money that we owe. When Emerson writes about debts, however, he extends the definition by including those less-than-obvious debts which, if we neglect or ignore them, may cause us difficulties.

First of all, Emerson believed that we all owe a debt to society, one that can only be paid by finding and living our purpose. For when we incorporate our purpose into our lives, society benefits from the fruits of our special calling. Whether grand or ordinary, each of our lives has the potential to enhance the lives of others.

If we look at the life of Nelson Mandela, for example, we see destiny in action. Not only has Mandela contributed greatly to society, but he has remained true to this purpose even while imprisoned. A major force in abolishing apartheid in South Africa, Mandela couldn't be swayed from his dream of freedom, even after years of oppression. In other words, no matter what hardships he endured, his purpose remained the same, eventually culminating in his recent rise to power.

The ability to hold true to your purpose, despite all odds, is a good indication that you are on the right path. And although Mandela's story is a very dramatic example of overcoming obstacles, there are many less dramatic, but just as powerful, examples to be found in the lives of ordinary people.

My Aunt Roz, now retired, came face to face with her purpose at the age of forty. Throughout her entire life, she had always wanted to be a teacher, but because of the Depression, World War II, and a limited family income, she had gone directly to work after high school, forgoing her dreams of college and teaching. Eventually, she achieved a degree of success in the business world, and was, by all practical standards "set for life." Despite her achievements, however, Aunt Roz never lost her desire to teach. As a matter of fact, it increased, inspiring her to quit her job at forty years of age—something rarely done in the 1950s—and go back to college, to become an exceptional teacher.

Although many people advised against it, my aunt followed her dream and is still teaching today—in the senior citizen home where she lives and without pay—even though she has been retired for many years. When speaking about her teaching career, she says how lucky she was to have been able to do what she truly loves and was meant to do.

We know that we are doing what we are meant to do if the desire for it continues, even though we go off in different career and life directions. For if a purpose is real, try as you may, you can't shake it from your consciousness. It will stay with you and try to get your attention, so that, like my aunt, you can fulfill your destiny.

When we are truly fulfilling our destiny, by living our purpose, we will feel excited by our work, not drained by it. We might often say as I do, "I would do this work even if I wasn't getting paid for it." Usually, it will touch people's lives in some way. But most of all, it will touch your own, making you a more giving and loving person, and inspiring you to grow, rather than stagnate.

If we do not discover our purpose, or worse, if we find it but refuse to implement it, we are, in a sense, defaulting on our contract with the Universe. This "breach of contract" results in wasted lives, and people going to their graves unfulfilled and discontented. (In chapter five, I will examine the importance of finding our life's purpose in greater detail, as well as its relevance to successful living.)

We often stumble upon our life's purpose through the development of our individual talents and abilities. After all, a talent is a gift from the Universe that comes with the instruction: Use. Do not abuse. When we neglect our talents and let them wither, we violate our contract with the Universe, and gradually disempower ourselves. Although we may not experience any major tragedy because of this violation, nevertheless, our potential is diminished.

During those barren years when I just dreamed about writing, instead of doing it, I noticed an emptiness deep inside me that crippled me both spiritually and creatively. When I finally began writing, the emptiness gradually filled itself with the joy of creativity, which sparked my spiritual growth. If, however, I slip back and avoid writing for a while, a little ache appears, reminding me of my debt to myself and to the Universe.

Our hearts contain their own system of debt and fulfillment. This requires attention and the same level of commitment we give to our other contracts. Difficult to ignore, our heart's debts make themselves known through our most cherished and intimate relationships. A mother's debt to her children, for instance, consists not in the things she does as much as in the love she gives. No amount of material things will make up for a heart that refuses to open to those who have a claim upon it.

When we withhold love or distort it out of resentment or bitterness, our heart dries up from underuse. Life often becomes bland and meaningless as we reap the results of our neglect, and perhaps abuse, of those whom life placed near to us. Our spouses, our parents, our children, and even our friends represent responsibilities, which, if not honored, can hurt us in many ways.

How many parents have felt the pain of their children's resentment and anger? The cruelty, indifference, and heartlessness we express toward our children will come back to us, until we finally pay the debt we owe them from the moment of their birth, and love them as we should have loved them in earlier years.

This part of the law of compensation also applies to those of us who consistently deny our parents the love and forgiveness they need. For as long as love is withheld, the person withholding it will suffer as well. Remember that any emotion we repress, even love, will subvert our best efforts and contaminate our lives. Now, this is not to suggest that we continue to place ourselves in abusive situations, but that we forgive our parents and love them in the best way we can. Sometimes, the best way means to love them from a distance. The important thing here is the love, both of ourselves and of our parents, which exudes healing rays to wounded hearts.

We know intuitively where our heart's debts lie, and we also know when we aren't honoring them. If we don't, life will let us know by some form of diminishment, either within ourselves or within our lives. Perhaps our passions won't be as consuming as before or our health and well-being will be compromised, or perhaps our relationships will become stale, as life tries its best to open our hearts.

Life presents us with many gifts along the way, which openhearted people know are best to repay. Emerson stresses this point by encouraging us to give to the world what we have been given, yet many of us live with a feeling of deprivation and hoard our treasures, afraid that giving them away will deplete our supply. In fact, the very opposite is true, for the giving of monies, love, support, care—or whatever—balances the books of our Universal accounts and keeps the energy flowing within our lives.

Suppose you have just received a windfall from some blessed source. No one would ever advise you to give it all away. But remember to give in some way to someone else, in order to preserve the delicate balance of give and take within your life. When I experience a financial breakthrough, I often give a bit of the money to a source or person who might need it. At other times, I give extra time and love to those in my life. Or I might surprise someone with a desired gift or an invitation to dinner. Our intuition knows what we need to give, as well as to whom.

As you can see, it's not always necessary to repay the specific person who gifted us. For instance, I have been blessed for most of my life with wonderful friends who have supported me through many difficult and wonderful times. Certain family members have been encouraging as well, especially my mother and my aunt, who have consistently blessed me with love and financial assistance. Although I always try to give back to them directly, I also try to honor their gifts by offering the same support to others in need.

Throughout my writing career, many people have bestowed upon me the gifts of inspiration, encouragement, and advice—sometimes when I needed it, even when I didn't. One special friend encouraged me to keep going at a time when I was ready to give up. She provided me with the use of her computer when I couldn't afford to buy one. She even gave me stamps and envelopes so I might send out my manuscripts. When I think about how to repay her, I also think about how I can give other writers—or creators in any field—some semblance of the help and support she gave to me.

These "laws" of compensation are not meant to punish us or to make our lives more difficult; instead, they are meant to help us evolve as both spiritual and human beings. Each day, we need to seize the myriad opportunities that enable us to honor our spiritual, emotional, intellectual, and creative contracts. We also need to remember to give back to the world that which we have received, in order to keep the scales balanced and our accounts reconciled. For if we do that, we will discover that instead of being restrictive, this way of life can free us to enjoy all the blessings the world has to give.

Beyond the Golden Rule

> Give and it shall be given you. . . . He that watereth shall be watereth himself.
>
> —"Compensation"

"Do unto others . . . ," "What goes around, comes around," and the term *karma* all express the law of compensation, which states that we can only reap what we sow. Although this universal law may seem somewhat punitive, it needn't be, not when we understand the beauty of the justice and harmony that operates in spite of us, yet because of us.

Quite simply, we must give love in order to get it, be a friend in order to have one, show mercy in order to receive it, and so on, throughout our lives. If something is lacking within our lives, we need only to express or embody that quality in order to receive some of the same. Although this law may seem simple in theory, it can be difficult for us to discern its execution in our lives and in the lives of others.

Many of us are often confused when we see selfish, cruel, and greedy people amassing more and more wealth. If the law of compensation is valid, then shouldn't they be destitute, rather than financially successful? Certain Eastern philosophies would explain away this seeming inequity by referring to our past lives. Perhaps the greedy, yet successful, person was generous and giving in a past life, and therefore is entitled to rewards in this one. Emerson, however, preferring to focus on this life, asks us to look behind the surface success to the barren and often impoverished soul underneath.

For example, a successful salesman I know has netted an incredible amount of money during the past sixteen years. The richest member of his family, Dale ensures his security by hoarding his money instead of spending it. Miserly with other people, as well as with himself, he gives as little as possible and is often seen eating at the least expensive restaurants. Although he could afford better, he always buys economy cars, sleeps in the cheapest motels, and wears the same clothes for years. In spite of his rather parsimonious behavior, his income continues to increase, along with his bank accounts and his ways to save money.

Recently, however, I had the chance to speak with Dale in depth, and I discovered that he is a most unhappy, unfulfilled, and fearful individual. At forty years old, he confessed to living a life that wasn't his own; he spoke about the futility of it. His money, he explained, did nothing to alleviate his financial fears, but almost increased them. "I look at everyone as if they are trying to get my money," he declared, "especially women. Why, I've never been able to marry because of this fear."

After speaking with Dale, I realized the truth of that much-quoted statement about middle age being when you reach the top of the ladder and realize it's against the wrong wall. People like Dale not only have their ladders against the wrong walls, they have their hearts and souls in the wrong places. With only the love of money to guide them, their inner life withers or never develops at all. Remember, the Bible didn't say that money was the root of all evil, but that the *love* of money was.

In the truest sense of the word, Dale and others like him aren't wealthy at all. For true wealth consists not only of money but of abundance and prosperity. These priceless possessions manifest throughout all the areas of our lives, whether it be in the quality and quantity of meaningful relationships, or in the richness of the inner life as evidenced by the love, wisdom, and peace of mind that floods our inner being.

Remember, universal laws are not black and white, nor are they always clearly understood. Sometimes, we may give in one area and get back in another. And yet sometimes we may receive from exactly the same area we give to, but not find fulfillment in what we receive because of inequities in other parts of our lives. For example, Dale's inspired efforts to make a lot of money may have earned him financial security, but not true wealth, success, or happiness. Unfortunately, his skinflint ways and ungenerous nature returned to him, not in regard to his money, but in his general lack of fulfillment.

And what about fame? Just look at the many individuals whose desire for fame becomes the driving force of their lives. For example, Marilyn Monroe's ambition netted her legendary status in the world of entertainment. In short, she gave one hundred percent of her energy to reach the top and received back equal and fair payment for her efforts. But what about the things she didn't receive, such as happiness and peace of mind? If the law of compensation is valid, we can assume that Marilyn may have been less than giving in other areas of her life.

The preceding illustrations teach us that we need to look beneath the surfaces of people's lives to observe the inherent justice of the Universe. In most cases, surface impressions are often clouded with illusions that distort reality. Sometimes the balancing effects of compensation are beyond our initial vision, especially when deciding whether we reap the wrongs we sow.

In his essay "Compensation," Emerson unequivocally states that we cannot do wrong without suffering wrong. Yet, what we see around us every day are people getting away with all sorts of things, from the most innocuous lie to the most heinous crime. How many criminals are never even brought to justice? What about them? And what about the person who consistently takes advantage of people, yet always seems to get away with it?

In his novel, *The Picture of Dorian Gray,* Oscar Wilde tells the story of a young, handsome man who, while having his portrait painted, wished that the portrait would change and age while he remained always the same. Of course, the vain young man received his wish and proceeded to indulge in a most hedonistic, decadent, and sometimes evil existence. Throughout all the years of Dorian's debaucheries, his face and body remained the picture of untainted youth. The painting, however, altered with each diabolical act, and became a most hideous portrait of this man's soul.

This classic tale illustrates so well where suffering really occurs. When we harm each other in any way, our inner being is affected, and rather than evolving to higher levels, we descend into lower and less enlightened states. When someone commits a murder, for example, the retribution is immediate and continuous within their heart and soul. Although we may not see the particular effect of the retribution, we can be sure that somewhere, somehow, life's scales are being balanced, and that sooner or later, justice will be served.

Sometimes, the law of compensation enables us to experience the same hurt we inflicted on another. When I was younger, I unthinkingly hurt some of the men in my life, without a bit of remorse. Later I experienced like hurts, which helped develop my compassion and sensitivity. "Now," I thought, "I know how those men felt."

Furthermore, when we hurt others, we often hurt ourselves by our very own hand. Remember that the Universal laws operate within us as well as without. In truth, there is no real separation between the two. This being the case, the divine or "higher" part of us may be what carries out the retribution.

When I look back over my life, I can see how forces inside me drew me to situations that ultimately balanced the scales of my life. A bout of arrogance, for instance, would be followed—though not always immediately—by my meeting a person who would behave in the same way toward me. Also, the "good deeds" I've performed led me toward equally beneficial meetings, providing me with whatever help I needed at the time.

When I really stop and take the time to help someone, even if I never see that person again, somehow, in some way, life will gift me with equal, if not enhanced, benefits. The love I've given has been returned to me in so many ways that I am almost overwhelmed by all the multifaceted expressions of it. Whether through friendships, my husband, or family members, love and generosity seem ever present in my life.

When people give with a sincere desire to help, that opens the channels of love between the parties involved and transmits the energy of our pure intention to the other person. The truth is, on some level, the other person knows if your "gift" has a hook in it or not. It's important to remember not to offer assistance only because of the good we'll receive in return. This attitude taints the spirit of giving, which ultimately generates more negative karma. If part of the package is manipulative, the recipient is sure to know it and the benefits may be denied. We may not want to admit it, but a part of us knows whether a gift comes with a price tag because of the uncomfortable feelings engendered during the exchange.

I know a woman named Meredith who constantly invites people over for dinner, always presenting them with a most sumptuous and elegant meal but conveying an expectation of a reward for her graciousness and generosity. For instance, if you don't immediately extend an invitation in return, she gets angry and lets you know about it in subtle ways. She also is highly offended if weeks go by and she hasn't heard from you. "After all," she'll say, referring to her dinners, "I go to a lot of trouble to keep in contact with you." Because she isn't giving freely, I always feel that I can't receive freely and have since refused many of her invitations. Meredith complains all the time about the ingratitude of her dinner guests, who, she squawks, never invite her over for even a cup of tea. If, however, she graciously offered her hospitality, just for the pleasure of giving, she would no doubt have countless invitations.

As we approach the twenty-first century, the law of compensation is alive and well, and operating in all of our lives. We are part and parcel of its operation, just by the nature of our essential unity. And because of this unity, when we give to others we give to ourselves, and when we hurt others we hurt ourselves. No escape is possible, and no escape is necessary, as we ponder the system of justice in the Universe, follow its dictates, and learn to make it work for us, rather than against us.

· 4 ·

The Fourth Secret
Discover the Joys of the Present

Man postpones or remembers; he does not live in the present, but with reverted eye laments the past, or heedless of the riches that surround him, stands on tiptoe to foresee the future. He cannot be happy and strong until he too lives with nature in the present, above time.

—"Self-Reliance"

Where do you spend most of your time? In the present, the past, or the future? If you are like most of us, you probably either obsess or daydream about the past and worry or fantasize about the future. Caught up in plans, lost in reverie, and concerned about things to come, we live our lives missing out on the most important moment—the present one.

Many ancient and modern-day sages have explored the subject of "living in the moment." Emerson tells us unequivocally, that happiness, power, strength, and fulfillment are found only here, in this day, in this moment. Yet, so many of us continually miss out on the joy of the present, while our minds pull us in every which way but now.

In Thoreau's classic book, *Walden,* he writes:

I went to the woods because I wished to live deliberately, to front only the essential facts of life, and see if I could not learn what it had to teach, and not, when I came to die, discover that I had not lived.

When I first read this passage years ago, I trembled with fear as I mulled over the idea of coming to the end of my life and realizing I hadn't lived. To me, this seemed like the worst tragedy that could befall anyone, so I determined to live life fully, as they say, seeking out every bit of excitement that I could find.

I looked everywhere for this excitement, this "life," as I called it, and found it glistening behind every corner. Romances, especially illicit and ill-fated ones, infused me with this "life." Fabulous career schemes taunted me with grandiose energy, while parties and glamorous nights on the town fed my hunger. Year after year, my self-created dramas left me tingling with adrenaline, and always ready for more. Although these images of glamour, money, and fame, drew me toward what I considered "living," in my frenzied search, I felt more dead than alive.

As I neared thirty, the smokescreen began to clear. I remember one drunken evening when my then-husband and I were dining out with a couple of excitement junkies just like us. The dinner was lavish, the wine expensive, the atmosphere glittering, and the conversation meaningless. I clearly remember contemplating the futility of all this, as I thought to myself, The only thing worth developing is the soul.

Looking back, I realize that moment was a turning point for me, one that led me in some subtle way to the life I am living now. I suppose, in a way, I was fortunate, because I had the opportunity to sample all the world has to offer, yet found it wanting. I also discovered what Thoreau really meant when he wrote about living and life. For since that time, I've come to know that joy is present in every moment, be it grand or ordinary, and that happiness resides within.

I still find it frightening to think about coming to the end of my life and not having lived. And when we go through our days worrying about the future or obsessing about the past, we are, in a very real sense, missing out on life.

Seize the Day

> Write it on your heart that every day is the best day of the
> year. No man has learned anything rightly, until he knows
> that every day is Doomsday.
>   —"Works and Days"

In the movie, *Dead Poets Society,* the teacher—played by
Robin Williams—exposes his students to *Carpe diem,* Latin for
"Seize the day," showing them photographs of students before
them who, like most of us, lived rather mediocre lives. "Make
your lives magnificent, boys," he tells them, as they ponder the
wasted potential of those they see before them. While watching
this movie, I pondered my own life and contemplated the value
of a single day.

In Emerson's essay "Works and Days," he turns his attention
to this theme of *carpe diem,* and warns us of the folly of wasting
one single day. Within each day lie countless opportunities for
growth, for love, and for developing our potential to its fullest,
yet people fritter away their lives, thinking they'll "do it tomorrow," until they run out of tomorrows and literally out of life.

I know many people who postpone acting on their dreams and
goals until "the time is right." An acquaintance of mine who says
she wants to open her own business has countless excuses as to
why she hasn't done it. Unhappy with her present life, Jill complains constantly and dreams about how things will be better
when she finally does what she wants to do. In situations like this
one, we have to ask ourselves if the person *really* wants to move
ahead on a dream or prefers to remain stuck in lethargic comfort.

Lethargy, also called inertia, has an energy all of its own.
More aptly called an absence of energy, inertia keeps us stuck
where we are, and prevents us from doing the things we really
want to do. In order to break this pattern, we first need to ask
ourselves why we might not want to move ahead. Fear of change
is the cause of most inertia. Because of it we keep to our "com-

fort zones" and do not put ourselves at risk. Before I began writing, I lived this "stuckness," procrastinating when it came to my dream; I talked about writing, rather than doing it. Luckily for me, however, about six years ago, someone shook me out of this half-sleep, thereby helping me become what I am today.

Right after my divorce, I accepted a temporary job in the library of a local corporation, until I could find the writing position I really wanted. After not working for seven years, I wanted to gradually ease back into the employment market and saw this job as a safe beginning. My intuition was right on, for not only did I find a safe haven, I also found a comfortable spot from which to dream about the day when I would finally "be a writer."

A year went by quickly in this little corner of the world, as I formed friendships and chattered away about my dream of writing books one day. One friend of mine, a wonderful man named Jack, listened intently to my ramblings about writing and encouraged me in my pursuits. The problem was, I only talked about writing and never actually did it. One day during lunch, Jack looked me straight in the eye and really let me have it! "Marianne, I am sick and tired of seeing you waste your life dreaming about writing while another year goes by. Before you know it, your whole life will have gone by, and you will leave this earth without ever attempting to make your dreams come true."

Jack's words, and the intensity behind them, started me thinking about my resistance to pursuing my dream. I then thought about all the other dreamers I knew who year after year postponed seeking to fulfill their dreams and their lives. I could go for a long time without seeing them, but when I did it would always be the same old story, "Well, I still haven't started my book—applied to school, looked for a better job—but I will, next year."

I realized that a part of us is afraid of achieving our goals. After all, our lives would then have to change. We might also have to take some risks, possibly fail or, worse yet, succeed. I'll never forget the friend who once told me "It's frightening to get what you want." In my own case, I realized that I was petrified of exposing myself through my writing, of being vulnerable to criticism and rejection. After all, the kind of writing I was contemplating doing would let everyone know who I really was. In short, my real self would have to come out of hiding.

After a few days of self-examination, however, I accepted my fears, and decided to move ahead with my writing. I keenly remember that the fear of not achieving my goal suddenly became greater than my other fears, which inspired me to begin. Jack's words and my own subsequent reflections affected me so strongly that I started writing articles soon after that meeting. And although it wasn't until a year or so later that my first article was published, I knew I was on my way, and will always be grateful to Jack for helping me break my pattern of lethargy and procrastination.

I've read many stories of people who never really lived fully until they learned they were going to die. Well, the truth is, we are all going to die, so we'd better get started making our dreams come true. So before you sit down to another night of television, ask yourself if there is anything else you'd rather be doing. Do you have a dream you've put on the shelf, or an important task you've put off completing, maybe for years? If so, shake off the cobwebs and get started on it right now. Your life is waiting for you.

Live in the Moment

> The one thing we seek with insatiable desire is to forget ourselves, to be surprised out of our propriety, to lose our semipiternal memory, and to do something without knowing how or why.
>
> —"Circles"

What does it mean to be truly alive? Does it mean desperately chasing after each new thrill or experience in the hope of another adrenaline rush? Or does it mean something else, something so simple, yet so elusive, that it constantly escapes us?

Many Eastern philosophies, such as Zen Buddhism, teach that the only way we can experience this feeling of "aliveness" is to let go of the mind's compulsive movement between the past and the future and concentrate on the present moment. This concept of "living in the moment" has almost become a cliché, yet most of us still don't know quite what it means or how to experience it.

For my recent wedding, I spent months planning and organizing every detail, enjoying the preparations immensely. As the day approached, however, I began worrying about absolutely everything. Would I be able to sleep the night before, would I have a good hair day, would my premenstrual weight gain show in the pictures, would the minister be on time, would I be able to say my vows without crying? In short, the chatter in my mind made sure that I was everywhere else but in the here and now, which took me away from the beauty and excitement of those wonderful days.

When the wedding day finally arrived, my mind went to work again, thinking about whether we would be there on time, how quickly we could get the pictures taken, and so on. When we entered the door of the historic inn where the wedding was being held, I was so preoccupied with distracting thoughts I didn't even see the beautiful floral displays decorating the various rooms. At this point, I stopped myself. I knew if I kept on like this, I would go through my wedding day without really living it. As I slowed down, and breathed deeply, I looked slowly around me and took notice of the furnishings, as well as the guests' faces. Concentrating on my body, I felt bursts of excitement run through me, and I became very aware of the floor under my feet and the bouquet in my hand. I brought my attention back to the sounds around me, such as the piano music and the chattering of the crowd. By centering myself in this way, I knew that I was really present and could fully experience this most important day.

When Emerson writes about our desire to forget ourselves, he refers directly to that experience of present moment living, in which we feel totally at one with everything around us. When existing in this state, we engage with life directly and lose our feelings of separation and isolation. During these moments, we are able to fully enjoy whatever process we are involved with, free from worrying about the end result. Spontaneity, freedom, and a sense of aliveness are ours, whenever we immerse ourselves in what lies before us.

Take for example, the moments in lovemaking when we seem to merge with our partner. All sense of time and space fall away, as a feeling of oneness and total well-being fills us. Free and alive, released from our body and our inhibitions, we can act with spontaneity instead of forethought. Hopefully, during lovemaking, our things-to-do list falls away, as do past fears and insecurities. When this does not happen—as many of us can attest to from time to time—we become spectators to the act, rather than participants in it because our minds are awhirl with observations and reflections.

Exercise can also bring us into the present moment, especially the highly aerobic kinds like bicycling and running. When runners speak about a "high," they are referring to this "in the moment" experience. After the initial resistance is dispensed with, the runner's body seems to drop away, causing him or her to become energized and totally absorbed with the process.

One of the interesting points about these immersions is that any moment or any activity will do. Whether watching a sunset alone or taking in a concert with thousands of other spectators, being totally present will transform that experience into one of true aliveness and joy. I sense that this is what Christ meant when he said that the kingdom of heaven is upon the earth, yet we do not see it.

In his essay, "The Over-Soul," Emerson speculates that we cannot foresee the future so we can learn to live in the present. Even with this gift from nature, however, we rarely reside in the present, and instead spend our lives worrying, regretting, and overplanning, instead of living.

For a few weeks last fall, I spent most of my time in the joy of present-moment living. From the instant I awakened in the morning to the time I fell asleep at night, I embraced each moment completely, creating what can only be called extraordinary—even mystical—days. Unfortunately, those days didn't last, for I soon returned to my pattern of mental diversions. When I reflect on that time, I wonder what it was that gave me so many rich and full days. Perhaps my meditations were deeper and more regular then, or perhaps my commitment to life was stronger and fuller; I really don't know. I do know that it was wonderful.

When I look back over my life, I regret that I missed much of it because my mind was elsewhere. I do remember, however, wondrous moments when I felt truly alive and at one with the world and everyone in it. During such moments, the beauty of a flower can enrapture us as much as a romantic interlude, and when we live this way, we know that we are touching the Eternal.

But What About Our Plans?

> To finish the moment, to find the journey's end in every step of the road, to live the greatest number of good hours, is wisdom.
>
> —"Experience"

Is there any greater definition of wisdom than this wonderful statement of Emerson's, which quite simply, gives us one of the major secrets of successful living? Yet, many of us resist this moment-by-moment way of living because of what we call "our plans for the future."

A friend and I were recently discussing how busy our lives had become, how we virtually raced through our days, hardly conscious of the world around us. When I suggested that we really needed to live in the moment, she replied, "Oh, but if you did that, you'd never accomplish anything! What about all my plans and dreams for the future?"

What my friend didn't understand was that "living in the moment" is different from "living for the moment." Living *for* the moment often means that we are "going for gusto" by indulging our every whim and pleasure. A living-for-the-moment person is usually not concerned with the consequences of his or her actions, and prefers instant gratification to delayed. As a matter of fact, a living-for-the-moment person abhors plans and schedules, and will do anything to avoid them.

Living *in* the moment, however, most certainly *does* include plans and schedules, but requires that we be totally focused when developing and executing those plans. Most of us allow our minds to wander all over the place when we are engaged in a task. For example, when working on a project, we may be thinking about what we have to do next or worrying whether we will complete this chore on time. Or perhaps we may ruminate over a nasty remark our boss made or the fact that the new guy we met didn't call yet. In any event, these distractions deplete our energy and distort our focus, making us far less efficient. On the other hand, when we direct *all* of our being to the work before us, we almost become one with the work, which energizes us with fresh ideas and renewed stamina.

Another trap is to postpone living until we achieve a desired goal. I've heard many women say they will do this or that when they finally lose some weight, when they find someone, they'll be happy, or they'll feel successful when they finally become a writer/entrepreneur/actor/vice president etc.

For instance, let's say you now work for a corporation, but want to open your own business in two years. While developing your strategies and plans, you will most likely be so caught up in your dream that you will begin to live completely in the future, rather than the present. You may constantly daydream about "how life will be" when you are finally an entrepreneur, while totally discounting the immediate days and moments.

Emerson teaches us that happiness or success does not lie in some future reality, but within every moment of our lives. When he tells us to "find the journey's end in every step of the road," he encourages us to bask in the joy that the fulfillment of our desires would bring us, even while working toward them. So instead of postponing happiness until you lose weight or meet that special someone, realize it now, for as the cliché goes, "Tomorrow may never come."

Furthermore, while working toward your goals, try to release your attachment to obtaining from society the "label" of your desired profession. Whether you want to be an entrepreneur, chef, teacher, writer, or enlightened being, realize that by working at your goal, the seeds of your desire are already germinating within you. Although the seed is not the plant, it contains its essence, and when we realize this, we can claim for ourselves the label we choose. After all, does a writer need to publish a book to be considered a writer? Wasn't Alex Haley a writer even during the time he received nothing but rejections? And aren't you already a spiritual being even though you are still working on your path? Remember, it is the act of doing something that makes a writer, entrepreneur, computer programmer, spiritual adventurer, or whatever, not an outside event or the testimony of others.

If we continually keep our focus on others or on some future achievement, we will soon find that when we arrive at our goal, we have only momentary satisfaction. For soon afterward, another goal takes its place, thrusting us once more into the future. I remember when publishing an article was the primary goal of my life. As a matter a fact, it was so primary that I sometimes neglected to enjoy the beauty that surrounded me. By focusing my attention entirely on this future goal, I missed out on many wonderful moments that are now gone forever.

When I finally published my first article, I was ecstatic and reveled in the achievement for about a day, perhaps, two. I almost immediately grabbed hold of my next goal, losing myself in fantasies about what life would be like when I published my first book. After a few months or so of this myopic style of living, I realized that life was going by, and I was missing it. At that point, I opened my eyes and began enjoying all the wonderful things in my life, as well as the publishing of my book. After this milestone, I am sure another goal will inspire me, then another, and so on; but I am also sure that I have learned to savor each step in the road and to keep my attention focused firmly in the present, even while planning for the future.

Each and every moment presents us with opportunities for growth, for joy, and for intimacy. You miss out on so much, not only when you are stuck in the future, but when you focus more on what you are going to say or do than on what is right before you.

Have you ever had the experience of speaking with someone who is not really there? Even though you seem locked in conversation, you can sense that this person's mind is on what to say next, rather than on listening to you. Or maybe you have been the one busily scanning your conversational repertoire while a friend, lover, or acquaintance pours out his heart to you. In both of these cases, no real intimacy can occur.

On the other hand, when absorbed in the present moment, we can listen to our companion completely, noticing every inflection, gesture, and tone of voice. Anything that distracts us from the other person inhibits intimacy and keeps the relationship stagnant. In order for relationships to grow, we need to listen and converse with full awareness. Anything less cripples the communication, and diminishes the relationship. Distractions like this occur even in our most passionate moments, diminishing our connection.

Often during intimacy, our minds become absorbed with the end result, rather than on the means to this end. Instead of focusing on the interaction before us, whether it be conversation, kissing, foreplay, or whatever, we mentally jump ahead, out of excitement or anxiety, to the point of climax. Our partners can sense this on some level, and may possibly resent it. Although the resentment may not be immediate or obvious, months and even years of this type of behavior can severely damage the relationship and prohibit any real intimacy from developing. If, however, we truly bring our whole being into the intimate moment, our partner can sense our absorption, and know that we are fully and completely there.

Whether in lovemaking or in life-making, Emerson teaches us that true fulfillment can only be found in the here and now. Never one to discourage the achievement of goals, he encourages us all to reach our potentials, but warns us of the dangers of missing out on the wonders of one single moment—one single day.

Appreciate Beauty

> The question of Beauty takes us out of surfaces, to thinking of the foundations of things.
>
> —"Beauty"

Beauty is all around us, though we do not always see or experience it. Captivated largely by external appearances, we often miss the beauty hidden within an unattractive facade or a painful moment. In order to detect the beauty that lies, as Emerson says, in "the foundation of things," we need to look beneath the surface appearance and the surface meaning.

A beautiful face or exterior of any kind can hide a multitude of sins, and an ugly exterior can overshadow great inner beauty. Emerson tries to encourage us to see with new eyes, to view any object as a whole, seeing both its inner and outer qualities.

Looking at the world in this way enables us to perceive the laws of nature that operate within both people and things. We see the harmony naturally present within a truly beautiful object, even if the exterior may not conform to our current perceptions of beauty. Certain people, for instance, who are not conventionally handsome or beautiful, may exude a sense of harmony, order, power, energy, and beauty from within. We often say of these people that they have an "aura" or "presence" and often they can still a crowd with a single word. They exemplify the truth that beauty emanates from deep within, from the harmony of our beings.

Even inanimate objects have deeper levels that can be glimpsed by the perceptive eye. A lovely vase, for instance, is made even lovelier when we recognize the spiritual qualities underlying its surface structure. If we can glimpse the attributes of God—such as beauty, harmony, peace, and order—within it, we can gain a sense of the object's deeper beauty.

Somerset Maugham stated this concept beautifully when he wrote, "Love the objects of the world, not indeed for themselves, but for the Infinite that is in them." When we look at the world in this way, our eyes—or more appropriately, our souls—connect with the divine essence that is ultimately a part of everything. This type of vision helps us become one with the object, thereby sensing our unity with the whole.

When caught up in the stresses of everyday life, we rarely connect with anything, and barely notice even the most obviously beautiful object or scene. While caught in rush-hour traffic, I try to remember to breathe deeply, look around me, and notice the beauty already there. On one such occasion, while observing the autumn sky at twilight, I was almost moved to a state of rapture by the vibrant colors of the fading horizon. I felt a deep sense of awe as I beheld burnished leaves on blackened branches, reaching toward the sky. Sadly, I had passed that way hundreds of times before, but had never noticed the beauty because of my anxiety about sitting in traffic. I've also failed to enjoy beautiful music playing on the radio because of my concern with getting home.

Momentarily throughout our days, we need to take note of all the beauty around us and to sense our oneness with it. For ultimately, within all we see, lies the greatest beauty of all, namely the Divine Energy, or God. When we perceive the beauty of the world in this way, we can truly experience the joy of living. And when we experience the joy of living, we will understand that beauty can also be present in the unhappy and difficult moments of our lives.

When I recently received some unhappy news, which greatly upset me, I wondered if any beauty could be found in such sadness. Suddenly, when I finally hit the depths of my anguish, a queer sensation of strength and power shot forth from deep within me, causing a momentary sense of awe. At that moment, I understood what Joseph Campbell meant when he spoke of the sublime, an elevated aspect of beauty that can be found in certain tragic and difficult episodes of life.

Webster's Dictionary defines the sublime as something of outstanding spiritual, intellectual, or moral worth, tending to inspire awe and an elevated sensation. When we are absorbed in difficulties or caught within a torrent of violent emotion, the sublime is present to transform anguish into power, and tears into strength and beauty. It is that energy, often called grace, which seems to rise up within us during difficult times, allowing us to harness the spiritual potential hidden within the situation. The highest form of beauty, it lifts us to an almost mystical state, causing us to recognize God in even the darkest moments. Courage, compassion, mercy, hope, and love are just a few of the sublime visitors that may emerge from within us during our most trying moments.

For example, many people have been inspired to take up great causes when this sublime element is present. One person may start a support group after the death of a spouse, while another may initiate legislation that could have prevented a child's death. Someone else, rejected and alone after a divorce, may decide to love more by volunteering for any number of worthy causes. Or, on a different level, yet another person may use pain and tragedy to open the heart and transform the soul.

Even caught within my own emotional whirlwind, I am often conscious of a part of myself that has the ability to get beyond the situation. The only way to reach this transcendent place, however, is to move fully into the sensations and emotions I am feeling. By descending into the darkness, so to speak, I can transform the energy, and emerge strengthened and inspired. If I run from the difficulty or the pain, as another part of me wants to do, I'll simply become stuck in the sadness or anger, and never experience the transforming power of the sublime.

In her book, *Living in the Light,* Shakti Gawain notes that each "negative" emotion has a flip side, which enhances our life on some level. For example, she associates sadness with the opening of the heart. Often when I am crying, I do sense my heart opening up as I feel great compassion for all of humanity. During these moments my anger and resentment seem to dissolve within the light of forgiveness. Truly these are beautiful moments that have the potential for transformation—if we live them fully.

Now, I am not suggesting that we wallow in our miseries, but that we experience them fully as they arrive and in so doing, transform them. When we wallow in an emotion, we are stuck in the middle of it, not moving into and through it.

Unfortunately, certain people enjoy pain and find a distorted pleasure in suffering, but this is not what I am suggesting. Rather, I am talking about finding that element of the sublime that exists within all of us and will help us emerge from our difficulties as stronger and more spiritually evolved beings. When we recognize and utilize this sublime element, we are then elevated to a higher state. Wallowing, on the other hand, keeps us in a state of weakness and helplessness, which can never be transformed unless we choose to go through the heart of it.

In every difficult situation, we have the choice to experience the beauty and power of the sublime or to drown in a pool of misery and helplessness. By recognizing that, as Emerson says, "Even in the mud and scum of things, something, something always sings," we can welcome the darkness as something that can ultimately help us on our journey toward higher consciousness.

Let Go of Control

> A little consideration of what takes place around us every day would show us that a higher law than that of our will regulates events; that our painful labours are unnecessary, and fruitless; that only in our easy, simple, spontaneous action are we strong, and by contenting ourselves with obedience we become divine.
>
> —"Spiritual Laws"

As I read these very words, I can feel my body releasing the tension that comes from trying to arrange my life exactly as I want it. The part of me that is caught up with forcing events, rather than just letting them happen, breathes a welcome sigh of relief at the possibility of a "higher law" regulating our lives. If I could only live as Emerson says—easily, simply, and spontaneously—the joys of the moment would not be lost, and paradise would be found, once again.

Linda Leonard, author of *The Creative Fire: Beyond Addiction,* calls us a society addicted to control. All we need to do to confirm that is to observe how our culture tries to organize everything into categories, systems, and "safe" patterns. For example, unemployment and disability insurance protect us against hard times, while the welfare system takes up the slack after these two have been exhausted. And when filling out forms or applying for jobs, our backgrounds—or lack of them—puts us into the categories from which we are judged. To "protect us," society has devised guidelines on how to behave socially, romantically, and professionally. Whether by bureaucracies, social systems, insurance coverages, financial plans, or just by simple rules and regulations, life is made secure and predictable.

I, of course, recognize the need for these various "safety nets," knowing that they can make life easier and more comfortable. The problem occurs when the impetus for these programs is a need to control, rather than a desire to enhance, life. For with "control" at the helm, our society cannot help but produce more and more do's and don'ts because of increased fear of the unstructured and uninhibited. In fact, the more we rely on a structure of any kind, the more fearful we are of losing that structure.

In our individual lives as well, we try to control and manipulate circumstances and people to suit our preferences. If a spouse doesn't act the way we want him to, we try to change him. If a certain situation isn't turning out the way we would like, we try to force it into shape. We even try to control our bodies with diets and exhaustive efforts to mold them into perfection. Often our emotions and natural impulses are put under "control" as well, resulting in all types of mental and physical illnesses. We even try to get our careers to submit to our wills, by using manipulative and so-called political tactics designed to help us "move up the ladder."

I've observed many people, including students of mine, who choose jobs or even their careers on the basis of "security," rather than on the basis of what they love. Goaded by their fears and insecurities, they try to take the question mark out of the future by opting for a "sure thing" financially.

Obviously, we must have goals in order to fulfill our potentials. We run into problems, however, when we let our egos run the show. For the ego concerns itself mostly with basic survival issues and is deathly afraid to release its control to a higher authority. Frightened of losing its hold on the events of one's life, the ego does everything to ensure that it remains the controlling force. Instead of the ego, we need to listen to that divine part of ourselves, which is based in love and spiritual growth. Frequently called the "higher self," this inner guidance system goes beyond will and ego, connecting us to the Over-Soul, or Universal Mind.

Sometimes this inner director may concur with our ego's plans and desires; at other times it may directly oppose them. One thing we can be certain of is that the higher self's plan is always for our higher good; the ego's plans, as many of us know, are not.

During the disintegration of my first marriage, I remember almost wearing myself out in a battle between my will and my higher self. At that time, my will consumed itself with holding on to my marriage, even though its destructiveness was well documented. Frightened of facing the future alone, I manipulated my husband and tried to force my way back into his life. As a matter of fact, I can't remember a time when my will was stronger.

Despite that, all my plans and manipulations failed, and my ex-husband went on to other things. When I look back over that time and think about the energy I wasted, it seems clear that a higher will was indeed operating and that this higher will had my best interests in mind. Since that time, my life has far surpassed anything I knew before, and I thank God that my efforts for reconciliation failed. Now, understanding the inordinate amount of energy and time I wasted in following my will, I try to "let" my higher self be my guide. For experience has taught me that the more I surrender to my inner power, the better my life gets. And instead of struggling and straining, I seem to flow with the currents of my life, rather than against them.

Many conventional religions teach their congregations to make life decisions by following the will of God, a personal God that exists somewhere outside of us, usually in heaven. In other words, God's will for us comes from outside of ourselves, which means we have to look without to find it. It seems to me that this concept of following God's will is a valid one, except for the fact that we are looking for God in all the wrong places.

Since Emerson believes that God resides within each of us, the will of God can only be determined by inner communion. When he speaks of "obedience," he is referring to the state of being in which we allow our lives to be directed by this inner guide. As mentioned before, we must meditate, follow our intuition, and learn to know ourselves in order to hear this divine voice from within. Sometimes, however, this voice makes itself known by feelings and impulses rather than by words.

Often when we speak about having a "feeling" about something, or we experience the need for a particular type of action, this inner guide is trying to make its wishes known. I often get a sick feeling in my gut when attempting to do something that goes against my inner guidance. Many times if I accept a project that I know is not right for me, my energy level quickly decreases and an almost gloomy feeling descends upon me.

During much of my life, ignorance and disregard of this inner voice has cost me, in terms of money, time, happiness, and spiritual growth. Lately, however, I've learned to be somewhat more spontaneous and to heed the call of my higher self. I remember an incident only a few years ago when I was at a pivotal point in my career and almost made the wrong decision. After answering an ad for a public relations job and landing an interview, I sat, one rainy afternoon, in the director's office, trying to convince her that I was the person for the position. I had also been offered a teaching post, something I'd never tried doing before, but the pay in public relations was great, the opportunities were substantial. Though the demands of this position would cut down on my writing time, the money would be far more than I was making in my freelance editing/writing career.

About halfway through the interview, however, an uneasy feeling began to stir inside me. Before I knew it, I was telling the public relations director that I didn't really want the job, I didn't like being in the business world, and I had decided to teach and pursue my writing career. Astonished by my honesty, the director thanked me for opening up to her, then suggested that we keep in touch.

Almost immediately, I felt a lightness within and knew that I had made the right decision. That spontaneous impulse to voice what I really felt saved me from choosing a career that would have led me in the wrong direction. For time has shown that my decision to teach—and to continue writing—was the right one.

These days, because of many experiences like the previous one, I am increasingly conscious of my inner guidance and more aware of its messages. If I take the time to listen and to hear what this inner guide wants, I can be sure that it will move me toward greater opportunities, both spiritually and otherwise.

And although I still have problems with control, I am perceiving, almost daily, the futility of that way of life. As I learn to let go and flow with events rather than rail against them, my consciousness is enhanced and I grow toward greater empowerment. The need for control brings us nothing but stagnation and frustration, while letting go frees us so we may evolve into the enlightened beings we were meant to be.

The Way to Fulfillment

> Place yourself in the middle of the stream of power which animates all whom it floats, and you are without effort impelled to truth, to right, and a perfect contentment.
>
> —"Spiritual Laws"

We enter this world as truly magical creatures whose absorption in the present moment turns life into a virtual paradise. Watch children at play and you can see how they delight in the smallest things, by making every moment their own. I've often envied the joy small chidren display for anything from the tiniest insect to the grandest amusement park. Granted, all these things are new to them, which partly accounts for their awe, yet there is something more, something intrinsic within the moment itself.

Before children become self-conscious, they exist within what Emerson calls "the stream of power," although they are not fully aware of its origin or potential. Remember that authentic power originates from our union with the divine source within us, as opposed to worldly power, which originates from such external sources as money, status, physical strength, knowledge, beauty, et cetera. As children, we spend much of our time within each moment, which is the only place where authentic power really lies. Because we have not yet been fully socialized, we lack the self-consciousness that often leads us to separate from the moment and from God. As the mind develops, however, we break away from this divine stream and learn to focus our attention instead on the outside world. It is then that we begin searching for the power we lost when we severed our connection with the Universe.

This search continues all of our lives, impelling us to acquire as many symbols of external power as we can. But whenever we attain yet another brass ring, we discover that we still feel powerless, which spurs us on the next quest.

Like most of us, I lost my connection with God at a young age, and grew up feeling utterly powerless and frightened of the world around me. At that time, a quiet yet potent commitment developed within me—to trade in this feeling of powerlessness for one of power. The first power trip I went on involved the allure of physical beauty; I relentlessly pursued a beautiful face and figure. After achieving my goals, I discovered that beauty was truly only skin deep, which lured me onward to pursue other exotic powers.

The next was alcohol, which seemed to transform my powerlessness into a heady strength. While I was under the influence, nobody knew that hidden inside of me was a fearful, anxious creature. To my fellow revelers, I provided entertainment and drama. I was known as the life of the party. Yet, in spite of that, my insecurity remained and spurred me on.

Next on my itinerary was marriage to a charming and successful young man. Well, my depleted power center cried, if I don't feel powerful myself, maybe someone else's force can counteract my own weakness. What I didn't count on was my husband's own feeling of powerlessness, which, combined with mine, sent us on treasure hunt after treasure hunt, gathering as many shiny jewels as we could find, in the vain hope that they might finally empower us.

Although my particular power trips may have been slightly different from yours, you probably recognize the pattern. Unfortunately, this cycle operates throughout most of our lives, until we finally appreciate the true power that exists within ourselves.

This authentic power flows freely, bringing order, harmony, and growth to all it touches. It infuses the entire cosmos, causing trees to grow, rain to fall, and the seasons to change. In other words, it animates whatever it comes in contact with, helping all that is touched to fulfill its potential, whether by producing apples or producing a play. When a tree produces fruit, it does so because it is connected to this universal power, which enables it to fulfill its destiny. When a man or woman produces a great work of art, the same principle is operating, bringing the individual into the arms of his destiny.

Remember that this "stream of power and wisdom" intends us to fulfill our destiny—and will assist us in doing so only if we place ourselves in its capable hands and let it work through us. The great men and women of history were really no different from you or me, except in one way. They allowed themselves access to this Universal Energy which impelled them in the direction that was most suitable to them; in fact, "to truth, to right, and a perfect contentment." And if we live consistently within this stream, our world will reflect the heaven that Christ said existed within us.

The first step on the journey toward paradise is to recognize this power source deep within the center of our beings. If we can feel it and understand its origin—on an intuitive, as well as an intellectual level—then we can make it work for us. Yet, in order to sense this power source, we first need to immerse ourselves within the present moment. For we can only sense this energy if we are awake enough to incorporate all of our awareness within the moment and not let our minds take us away.

The best way to center the mind in the moment is to meditate. To meditate simply set aside fifteen to thirty minutes of quiet time daily for practicing breath awareness. To begin with, take four or five deep breaths and really feel the air going in and going out. Then for the remainder of the time, breathe naturally, but keep your focus on the inhalations and the exhalations. If extraneous thoughts come up, allow them entry, while bringing your attention back to your breathing. That's it.

If you meditate like this each day, you will soon find that your mind is being "retrained" by this process. For what this simple, but profound, breath technique does is retrain your mind to keep its attention in the present moment. Obviously this takes time, but if you are consistent, you will find yourself spending more time in the here and now. You will also notice that your mind is clearer, your energy increased, your stress level diminished. At the same time, your connection with God and the world is strengthened.

We can also center ourselves throughout each day, by practicing awareness or "mindfulness" as it is sometimes called. For instance, if you find yourself "stressed out" and your mind is racing in many directions, you can inwardly stop yourself and begin focusing on the sights or sounds around you. Whether you choose the pencil on your desk, the music on the radio, the stain on the wall, or your co-worker's voice, really absorb yourself in it. Keep your attention on one thing at a time, noticing how this one-point focus pulls your mind back to the present. Unfortunately, when one is in the midst of tension, the mind is being pulled in every direction, when what it really needs is to ground itself in the energy of the moment.

After we connect with this energy, we need to *keep* our attention in the present, for if we disconnect from the moment, we also disconnect from our power source, which casts us back to the world of the unempowered and unfulfilled. Obviously, staying consistently in the moment is challenging and difficult to accomplish. However, we owe it to ourselves to practice moving deeper and farther into the here and now, while at the same time accepting our inability to sustain it. For the more we live within this stream of power, the better our lives will become.

Knocking on Heaven's Door

If we will not be marplots with our miserable interferences, the work, the society, letters, arts, science, religion of men would go on far better than now, and the heaven predicted from the beginning of the world, and still predicted from the bottom of the heart, would organize itself, as do now the rose, and the air, and the sun.

—"Spiritual Laws"

The words "miserable interferences" of life typically conjure up images of rush-hour traffic, ringing telephones, tiresome people, and so on, but Emerson recognized the most miserable of all: the mind. As many sages throughout history have discovered, the mind can be both a blessing and a curse. For although it can lead us toward great realizations and ideas, it can also keep us from being in the moment, and ultimately from God.

When our minds run the show, they can keep us isolated from ourselves and from each other. Coming into the moment requires dropping the mind and acting from the spontaneity and intuition of the heart. Of course, we need analytical and critical thinking skills in order to put our impulses into practice. But too often the mind takes center stage and diminishes the intuitive side, without which we cannot be whole or happy.

The thinking mind seems to continually draw us back to that part of the self which compulsively seeks fulfillment from outside itself, thereby creating a separation between us and the world, and leaving us unfulfilled.

So do we suppress or destroy this mind, which continually causes us to feel separate and often isolated? Interestingly enough, Shunryu Suzuki, author of *Zen Mind, Beginner's Mind,* suggests the opposite: "You should be grateful for the weeds you have in your mind, because eventually they will enrich your practice." Instead of fighting the mind, we should accept its frenetic wanderings. For only by accepting them can we hope to transform them into our servants rather than our masters.

Acceptance can also help bring one back into the moment when faced with a difficult problem. If I am upset about something, my mind steps into what I call "the field of chaos" and starts obsessing and creating fears about the situation. When locked in this state of mind, I walk around with a glazed look in my eye, completely out of touch with myself and the world around me. It is during these times that I may lock the keys in the car, slam my finger in the door, run a red light, or do any number of destructive things. After each of these disasters, my mind flies farther off the beam, until I finally stop myself and apply the healing balm of acceptance.

When I look at my problem clearly and accept the reality of the situation, my mind stops catastrophizing and calms down. A deep acceptance brings me smack into the moment again, where

I can deal with my problems effectively. A chaotic state of mind only creates more chaos, which leads me farther away from the moment and from a solution.

It is tempting to look to the future for relief from our problems, but avoiding the present only means postponing the problem, not successfully dealing with it. Remember that it is what we ignore that ultimately controls us. And whether that something is physical pain, an unpaid bill, a relationship difficulty, or a destructive emotional pattern, we'd better deal with it now, rather than let it fester into something much more difficult and formidable.

Often, we seek relief from our problems by reading books such as this one, hoping to find the secrets to life itself. Secrets may indeed be discovered, but they should come with a warning label: be careful of living too much in the mind, rather than in the heart. For although the ideas in books can be valuable and transformative, too much emphasis on mental capacity can close the door to the heart and to experience of the divine.

Early in my spiritual path, I fell prey to what can almost be called an addiction to spiritual material. I read every book I could on the subject, attended many workshops, and listened to countless tapes, with the hope that my enhanced intellect would save the day. In other words, instead of concentrating on my heart, I concentrated on my mind.

It is through the heart that we find the joy of the moment, and it is through the joy of the moment that we find our hearts. If we remember just this one idea and live it daily, we shall discover that heaven is not a place but a state of mind when the heart is open.

If so basic to human experience, why then isn't this living in the moment more common? Krishnamurti suggests that society doesn't encourage being in the moment because then people would be more difficult to control, for society can only shape and condition us through our minds. When we are in the present moment, we step beyond the mind, which means beyond our social conditioning, and into our authentic selves. And when we are authentic, we live from our inner guidance system, rather than from any externally imposed one.

Sometimes in life, the simplest things are the most difficult, yet the most precious. Although living in the moment may sound easy, because of our conditioning it often takes a lifetime of practice to achieve. Nevertheless, it is well worth the effort, for when you experience truly being in the moment, you will find that the joy you discover leads you directly to life, and to God.

· 5 ·

The Fifth Secret
Find Your Life's Purpose

There is a persuasion in the soul of man that he is here for cause, that he was put down in this place by the Creator, to do the work for which he inspires them, that thus he is an overmatch for all antagonists that could combine against him.

—"Courage"

Many of us today are still struggling to discover our "perfect" career, which we hope will lead us to our purpose in life. Emerson, too, encourages us to find and to do what some spiritual teachers call our "right work." If we read him carefully, however, we become conscious of yet another purpose—one that doing our "right" work may lead us to, but more importantly one that, if achieved, will help us fulfill our destiny.

The question of destiny occupied much of Emerson's thought throughout his life. To him, our destinies included the work we were meant to do, as well as the persons we were meant to become. But more importantly, it included achieving the most important purpose of all: a union with God. Oftentimes, like many other spiritual seekers, he looked to nature for assistance, taking long walks in the woods hoping to ignite this universal oneness.

Whenever I feel disconnected from the God source within me, I too "take to nature," and wander through the forests near my home in search of some wisdom. After a while, my problems seem to fall away, as I begin to understand nature's message and to comprehend what our ultimate purpose is in life. All the trees seem to whisper it, confirming the echoes of my heart, which usually by then has but one goal, to be at one with God. This revelation always seems to put my worldly concerns into perspective. Then I understand what Emerson knew, that our highest purpose in life is to discover our God nature and live it completely. Period. Although other purposes may call us, discovering our right work being one of the most important, the primary purpose that brought us all to this earth is to unite once again with the Infinite of which we are all a part.

My experiences have taught me that this "oneness" almost always leads you to the work you were meant to do, and to any other person, place, or thing that will help you fulfill the perfect expression of your God nature. Secondary purposes such as raising children, providing help in the community, creating beautiful environments, or educating others, to name a few, will all fall into place as we live more and more within this oneness.

Furthermore, if you are living in this oneness, and following its impulses, you cannot help but be compelled to whatever or whomever reflects your essential nature. I especially love Emerson's words in "The Over-Soul": "The things that are for thee will gravitate to thee." Emerson encourages us to cease from our desperate search for this or that, knowing that because like draws like, we will be brought face to face with all that we need for our spiritual fulfillment. Minor examples of this phenomenon present themselves throughout our days, and include anything from finding a book that speaks to the soul to finding a home that perfectly meets your needs and expectations. As a matter of fact, the home I am living in now wonderfully illustrates the validity of Emerson's theory.

When my husband and I started to look for a house, we soon discovered that it would be difficult to find a suitable place within our price range. Discouraged, we put the search on hold for a while, intending to come back to it within a couple of weeks. During those weeks, however, some friends learned that their longtime tenants were moving out, and asked us if we would like to take the place. Amazingly, the price was exactly right, and the residence was beautiful. Located within a lovely, country setting, it was a charming and separate addition to the owners' eighteenth-century farmhouse. Within a month, we moved in and are still enjoying this lovely home, which seemed to come to us from out of nowhere.

What still amazes me is that we hadn't even really started our search when this opportunity came about. As a matter of fact, we weren't actively looking; we were "resting" in a state of faith and oneness.

Experiences such as this one have shown me how easily things come to us when we are immersed in wholeness, rather than fragmentation. I'd always suspected that life was not meant to be as difficult as we make it, although I never knew the reason why. I have learned that many difficulties and problems occur because we are divorced from our spiritual natures much of the time and caught up in our physical and material desires. If we lived consistently within that divine part of ourselves, our lives would be significantly easier and less stressful.

Obviously, it is difficult to remain in this state for very long, although certain people do. Unfortunately, our conditioning pulls us away from this blissful state more often than we would like. Even now, my moments of union are sporadic and hard to come by; yet I know that they are worth pursuing at all costs, for within these moments lie the doorway to heaven.

When we reach this "promised land," and make our residence there, we discover that all roads lead to this one. We also discover that by reaching this final destination, all our other purposes in life become clear, directing us to that which we are meant to do, and to be.

More Than a Career

Slow, slow to learn the lesson, that there is but one depth, but one interior, and that is his purpose. When joy or calamity or genius shall show him it, then woods, then farms, then city shopmen and cab drivers, indifferently with prophet or friend, will mirror back to him its unfathomable heaven, its populous solitude.

—"Considerations by the Way"

On the road to discovering our purpose, we often get side-tracked. After all, what if you have many interests or talents and can't choose between them? And what if you actually have no idea what kind of work you are meant to do? Or if you are quite content to do whatever job comes your way? Does this mean that the likelihood of discovering your purpose is slim? Of course not. What it could mean is that you need to expand your idea of what a purpose actually entails.

For example, a multitalented friend of mine spent many frustrating years trying to choose among her many careers. Not only is she a writer and producer, she also enjoys working in public relations, acting, painting, and business. As a matter of fact, it seems that Susan is constantly coming up with new ideas to implement and develop. For most of her life, she agonized over which one of her many activities was the "right" career, but could never seem to decide. Then one day, she called me and told me she had finally discovered that her purpose was multidimensional and it included anything and everything that would add joy, ease, and enlightenment to people's lives.

After considering Susan's revelation, I realized that I, too, had been limiting my purpose, so I set out to discover whether I could expand its scope and vision. First, I decided to meditate on it and came up with "to love and enlighten through speaking and writing." Instead of limiting myself to just being a writer or a teacher, this revelation helped me to bring my purpose into all areas of my life.

For example, I see my purpose being fulfilled whether I am offering some kind words to a friend or writing a thank-you note. Helping students with their difficulties is another way of living my purpose, as is writing this book. For as long as I am offering some form of love and enlightenment, my purpose is being accomplished.

If you want to discover your "greater" purpose in life, try going within and asking your intuition for help. Set aside a special meditation time just for this "purpose," and silently state your intention before you enter into the meditative state. In other words, as soon as you sit down and close your eyes, say to yourself "I desire to know my purpose in life," or something to that effect. As you relax and move deeper into the world within, ask your intuition to let you know what your purpose is. Then listen and grab hold of the very first thing that comes to your mind. Don't try to deny or analyze the answer, just keep asking until some pattern emerges. When you feel ready, open your eyes and write down what the predominate message was. Take this statement and see if it fits into the scheme of your life. Does it seem to resonate from deep within you? Is there evidence in your life that would point to this purpose? And lastly, does it feel right to you? For if it is truly your purpose, then you will experience a deep inner knowing about the truth of this statement.

If you still want further validation, ask God or your higher power to let you know if you are on the right track. Then forget about it and watch the answers appear. You may pick up a book that confirms or adds to your findings, or a friend may say something that will help clarify your experience. In any event, be open to anything that seems to help you define this all-important question of your life.

Obviously, a specific career may be part of your purpose, but most always, it will speak more about the qualities of life, than the specifics. A wise student of mine once referred to her purpose as being similar to the "mission statement" of an organization, which attempts to define its higher-level aims and goals. For example, XXX Company's mission statement may go something like this: With total integrity and commitment to quality, we aim to manufacture products that will add pleasure and comfort to people's lives.

If we take the time to discover our higher purpose, we won't limit ourselves by focusing solely on career. By seeking to expand our understanding of our purpose, it can be fulfilled in various dimensions of our lives. For instance, if you feel that you are meant to be a mother, you may find upon meditation that your deeper purpose is to nurture, love, and enlighten children. If this is the case, then your purpose would be served not only with your own child but any other, which could lead you to bring those needed qualities into many children's lives.

Of course, there are those who say that our only real purpose here on earth is to love, period. Obviously, this is true and should be part of any purpose. Nevertheless, we need to define our own purposes as best we can and live them to the fullest. For you can be sure that as you evolve, your purpose will evolve as well, bringing you new and greater levels of fulfillment.

As we start chipping away at our purpose, it will emerge in greater levels of depth and clarity. As Emerson says, all life will mirror it back to us, reaffirming to us that we are on the right path. Synchronicity plays a part in all this, bringing us messages from friends or foes alike about what we are to do. When I was confused about the direction my life would take, I remember turning on the television and being struck by a line in a movie, "You must first be empty in order to be filled." A day later, I casually picked up a book, and read the same words, "You must empty yourself before you can be filled." As I pondered the coincidence, I realized that I needed to empty myself of many of my limiting beliefs, ideas, and misconceptions, before I could truly discover my purpose.

The clues to our purpose are everywhere, once we make the effort to begin looking. They may be hidden in the pages of a book, the words of a friend, or within nature's whisperings. The real key, however, lies within ourselves. The best we can do is gather up the external clues and take them within ourselves for clarity and explanation. This clarity may come sooner, or it may come later, but it will come, if only we make the effort to forage through our internal chambers.

Finding Your Purpose is not Inevitable

> We see young men who owe us a new world, so readily and lavishly they promise, but they never acquit the debt; they die young and dodge the account; or if they live, they lose themselves in the crowd.
>
> —"Experience"

Sadly, many of us just simply do not find our purpose. Some of us may go through our entire lives without even a thought of what we are here for. Others may follow the calls of security and money, believing that our purpose consists only in making "a good life" for ourselves and our family. And then there are those unfortunate few who discover their purpose, yet never fulfill it.

The fast pace of life today, with its obsessive focus on externals, leaves little room to contemplate our reason for being. People frequently follow mindlessly a pattern of going to school, getting married, and having a family, without even a thought to any deeper meaning. When I ask my students, most of whom are college freshmen, what they want to do with their lives, they usually tell me that they want to get a good job in their chosen field and eventually marry. The thought of any purpose beyond these conventionalities barely enters their minds; perhaps because their parents—and society—have so narrowly focused their perceptions. I know when I was growing up no one ever talked about anything as important as a purpose. A job and marriage, yes; a secure and financially successful life, by all means; but never a purpose.

Unfortunately, this type of narrow vision leads us down the path of job, family, house, and retirement, while often neglecting our spiritual growth and the fulfillment of our destiny. Though religion may play a part in this typical scenario, it is often focused solely on our "good behavior" and on the afterlife. In contrast, when we live life with our purpose in mind, we may wander down the same path, but with the light of awareness. Connecting with this deeper level of consciousness will transform many elements of the typical pattern of job, family, home, retirement, and religion, and will infuse our whole life with meaning. In other words, these life patterns will enhance our evolution and spiritual growth, rather than diminish them. Instead of just mindlessly wandering through the avenues of life, we will think about what we are doing, why we are doing it, and will ask ourselves if that fits in with our purpose.

For example, at retirement, we will take stock of our life, and really think about how we want to live in the future. We will ask ourselves questions about the quality of our life, its spiritual significance, and think about how we can contribute to society in the coming years. We may also think about death and make a decision about how we want to make that transition. In short,

we will continue to live a conscious life rather than a programmed one.

And conscious living calls upon us to utilize all of our potential, not just some of it. For just as we use only a small percentage
of our brain's capacity, we also use only a small percentage of
our soul's capacity by neglecting the "sole" reason it came to this
earth. Whatever our soul's purpose, it needs to be fulfilled or we
will die without accomplishing what we were born to do.

At the end of Emerson's essay "Worship," he writes that dying
will not release us from completing our purpose. Without specu-
lating about the exact nature of the afterlife, he suggests that our
soul's task is meant to be completed, and will continue on its
journey until that task is fulfilled.

Remember, our purpose needn't be anything monumental or
fame producing; we are not all meant to be a Mother Teresa or a
Martin Luther King, Jr. Our purpose may be something as simple and as profound as helping people lead more comfortable
lives, which might be accomplished in any number of ways, including such diverse careers as masseuse or auto mechanic, or by
creating a loving home for friends and family to enjoy.

When you are aware of your purpose, housekeeping or working in McDonald's can be a way to fulfill yourself, rather than a
symbol of shame and servility. From this perspective, an accountant can be dedicated to helping people bring order into their
lives, while an interior decorator can add beauty to the world.

When you are in touch with your purpose, you can express it
in many ways, knowing that they may change as you grow and
develop. The purpose of some people is served by having various
jobs throughout a lifetime, others just by having one. The essential ingredient is that we realize what we are here for and then
bring that purpose into every area of our lives, whether it be our
homes, our jobs, our relationships, or our spiritual lives.

After we discover our purpose, we then have the choice to live
it or not. Because of the effort involved, many well-intentioned
people choose not to live out their purposes, even when they
know better. After all, it does take energy and commitment, both
to discover our purpose and to live it out. For instance, we might
have to leave a particular job or relationship because it does not

reflect our true identity, then face financial or personal insecurity for a while. Such a choice requires courage.

The road to fulfillment is often paved with obstacles, as well as blessings. Many of us feel that once we find our purpose, the road will then be smooth, direct, and free of problems. Although your life will probably improve once you do find your purpose, this does not mean there will be no challenges to overcome. As Emerson writes in "Compensation," difficulties often appear to help us grow to the next level of consciousness. When faced with an obstacle, we need to discern the possible reason for its appearance and then decide what we need to do to turn the obstacle into an opportunity. Viewed this way, stumbling blocks can be transformed into the stepping stones that will help us to evolve.

Although our purpose will probably remain essentially the same throughout our lives, it too can evolve along the way. For instance, I've often had the desire to return to interests which, years ago, brought me a great deal of fulfillment and pleasure. Looking back on my life, I can recall wonderful days of painting and playing the piano; they seem to stand out now amongst a sea of worldly pleasures. One day I will most likely return to these pursuits and incorporate them into my purpose in life, extending my original purpose—to love and enlighten through beauty of expression in writing and speaking—to include both painting and music.

In Ernest Hemingway's story *The Snows of Kilimanjaro,* an old man tells his nephew, a frustrated and unfulfilled writer, about a puzzling discovery. At the western summit of snow-covered Mt. Kilimanjaro was found the dried and frozen carcass of a leopard. No one knows what the leopard was seeking at that altitude, but, the uncle suggests, if the writer can figure it out that may save his life.

Instead, a minor character solves the riddle by innocently stating that it may be the leopard "took the wrong path and got lost." Like the dead leopard, many of us have lost our way and are in danger of dying a spiritual death because we have chosen the wrong path and are not fulfilling our purpose. For by not fulfilling our purpose, we cut ourselves off from God and from ourselves. By taking the time and effort to find the right path, we can begin to fulfill the destiny that is uniquely ours.

Choosing Your "Right" Work

> Each man has his own vocation. The talent is the call. There is one direction in which all space is open to him.
> —"Spiritual Laws"

In the eighties, many of us concentrated on success, rather than on fulfillment. Visions of wealth and position drove us to ignore our inner leanings and to sell out to the highest bidder. But our obsession with money eventually left us high and dry, creatively and spiritually and in some cases financially. In the nineties, those of us disillusioned with the success patterns of the past have struck out upon a new search: the search for our right work.

Our right work means the vocation that uniquely reflects our inner blueprint of talents, interests, and purpose. So we ask ourselves: What kind of work was I put on this earth to do? Should I be a painter, an accountant, a parent, a pilot, or a construction worker? Who am I anyway?

Discovering our right work usually takes a great deal of time and effort. With all the choices today, we often find ourselves wondering "what we want to be when we grow up." Nevertheless, there are those lucky few who knew what they were meant to do almost before they could speak. Apparently, Napoleon knew he would be emperor, Pavarotti knew he would be an opera singer, and my cousin Lisa knew she would be a mother, much earlier in life than I had a clue about my "perfect" career. Over the years, I imagined myself a nurse, a reporter, a concert pianist, an actress, and a movie producer, not necessarily in that order. But luckily for me, most of these ambitions lost their appeal after I looked at them clearly—without the glamour—and realized what achieving them would entail.

Like me, most people need to forage a bit to unearth their destiny. Unfortunately, also like me, many folks are so cut off from their true selves that they barely know what they think let alone what work they want to do. Yet even with this barrier, a little glimmer of truth gets through now and then, to whisper directions to us in the hope that we will listen.

Looking back, I can recall that my desire to be a writer surfaced from time to time, in between all my other dreams, hoping to get my attention. Although I never seriously took pen to paper until my early thirties, this inner voice did inspire my enrollment in a graduate program in English Literature, because as it told me many times, The best training for a writer is to read great books. It was still years before I knew myself well enough to sense what I really wanted and to develop my talents.

Many talents surface throughout our lives. We may be blessed with a musical gift, as well as an aptitude for the law. Obviously, we can't fully develop every talent, so we have to choose. But how? Emerson tells us that "the talent is the call." But what talent? To this, I would respond by telling you to choose the talent that stands out the most. In other words, what is it you are most gifted in? With some people, this talent appears early on, as in Mozart's case, leaving no doubt as to what career direction to take. With others, the talent develops as they grow, leading toward an eventual realization of the appropriate career. While in many, the main talent may lie buried or repressed because of various personal or environmental causes.

For example, suppose you showed an aptitude for painting in first grade, but your teacher severely criticized some of your favorite pieces of work. If you painted the tree pink and gave the elephant two legs instead of four, well, chances are you would be corrected, especially if your teacher preferred paintings based in reality. If the response from the teacher was too severe, just that one incident would be enough to prevent you from ever painting again, and would cause you to submerge the talent.

When most of us were growing up, creativity was often discouraged, causing our talents to "run for cover." Most middle-class parents focus on so-called "practical" careers and steer their children away from anything "artistic." This conditioning often diminishes or exterminates creativity, causing people to go into careers which just don't fit them.

I too came from a family steeped in the values of security and practicality. In my case, however, the real damage was done by a teacher in grammar school who absolutely trashed one of my stories and told me I couldn't write. I remember being so excited about writing this particular story that I couldn't wait to hand it in. The teacher, unfortunately, had other ideas, and completely destroyed any confidence I had in my writing. After that incident, my writing ability, rough as it was, went undercover, and remained hidden away until I reached my thirties.

In the essay "Spiritual Laws" Emerson suggests a way to uncover these hidden talents and work them into a blueprint that could point us to the right work. What he asks us to do is to scour our memory banks for those incidents, stories, character traits, and people that seem to stand out from the others in our lives. For example, when I look back over my previous marriage, what leaps to mind are the times I spent writing, painting, and playing the piano. I remember one day in particular when I did nothing but move from one of these activities to the other, blissfully enjoying all three. Emerson would say that these memories—the ones that stand out among all the others—are clues to the discovery of my primary talents and desires.

For example, other dominant memories I have include writing a play when I was about nine years old and then performing it for friends and family, and writing many letters to family members that would often bring them to tears. Certain movies and books have always stuck in my mind. As a matter of fact, my love for literature is an important part of my memory bank, as is my eventual schooling in it. When reading certain books, I remember absorbing the images, words, and stories I found within them, as well as being inspired by the talents that produced them.

OK, so what do you do with this collage once you have it? First of all, Emerson tells us to allow these memories their emphasis, even if they seem out of proportion to the other events in life. For by pulling together all these reminiscences, we can come up with a composite sketch, so to speak, of our right work.

When doing this in your own life, let your intuition guide you back over your past in search of your fondest memories and peak experiences. Try to recall the times when you were engaging in something totally blissful. At what moments in your life were you the happiest? What were you doing then? Also focus on the events that seem to have had the greatest impact on you. Why did they have such an effect? Was there a sense of inner knowing during these moments? What did it reveal to you? Be sure to write down all of these memories, in the order of their importance, if possible. After you are finished with that, make a list of your deepest desires, the ones that stir your heart and seem to remain with you throughout all the changes of your life.

After you have made your lists, examine them, and group together any items that seem similar. Putting the puzzle together may be challenging, for all the pieces may appear to be disjointed and unconnected. What we need to do is look for the common thread that runs through our lists. As always, use your intuition. Draw pictures if you like. Do anything in order to reveal a pattern. Do you sense an artistic bent developing or a scientific one? Or does a fascination with business or finance appear? Is service to the community involved in any way? Is helping others an aspect that seems to recur? Do your memories place you alone or with people? Again, use intuition to spark more questions and reveal the answers.

After a while, a pattern should emerge that relates directly to your right work. Most often, what we see first is a general purpose, such as "loving and nurturing children." From this larger picture, we can often deduce a specific career or careers that may suit us. For example, you may choose to express your purpose of "loving and nurturing children," as a mother or father, a teacher, a guidance counselor, or a writer of children's books. For some of us, only one career will be evident, such as international finance or chemistry.

When I looked at my collage of memories and desires, I discovered that a general love for words, stories, beauty, inspiration, spirituality, and ideas presented itself. My lifelong desire to write and communicate fit in nicely with my peak memories, helping me translate my list into the work I am doing now.

This particular exercise can be fun, as well as fulfilling, and may provide you with some important discoveries about yourself and your destined career. Think of it as a treasure map that will, if you follow the clues and connect the dots, lead you to one of the greatest treasures you can find—the fulfillment that comes from your right work.

Work in the Right Direction

> Self-trust is the first secret of success, the belief that, if you are here, the authorities of the universe put you here, and for cause, or with some task strictly appointed you in your constitution, and so long as you work at that you are well and successful. It by no means consists in rushing prematurely to a showy feat that shall catch the eye and satisfy spectators. It is enough if you work in the right direction.
>
> —"Success"

A few months ago, I ran into an old friend I had not seen for a long time. After I joyfully caught her up on what I was doing and how much I loved my work, she sheepishly confessed that she was unhappy with her career as a successful insurance executive. "Why don't you take the time to find out what you really like to do," I suggested, quite innocently. At that, she got very upset and told me this was easy for me to say, because I didn't have children, or an expensive apartment, or car payments, or a certain lifestyle, but she couldn't possibly leave her job and change careers at forty years of age. Besides, she said, she didn't have a man as I did to take off some of the financial pressures.

Surprised at her reaction, I suggested that there is always a way to change your life, even at forty, if you are willing to make the effort, and some sacrifices. Unfortunately, that just seemed to make things worse, and she reiterated angrily the reasons she could not start the search for her right work. Eventually, I realized the futility of my attempt, and quickly took my leave.

After that meeting, I looked at my life with critical eyes, to see if any of her accusations were true. I reflected on how I had chosen to keep my expenses down so that I could write. I lived with my mother for a while and drove an old car, which I had just finished paying off. I took no vacations, bought very few clothes, had hardly any furniture. Granted, my standard of living has since improved, and yes, having a loving husband has certainly enhanced my life; nevertheless, for six years I lived a no-frills lifestyle so that I could continue with my writing and teaching. Not having children to support certainly made it easier on me, but that too was a choice I had made so that I could put all my energy into my life's work.

The point to all this reminiscing is that any one of us can begin doing our right work at any time, under any circumstances, if we are willing to make a little effort. Although I am not denying that family responsibilities make it more difficult, there are always ways to start on the path to career fulfillment.

First of all, as Emerson notes, we need to trust in the idea that we are all—and that means everyone—here for a purpose. By calling self-trust the first secret of success, Emerson stresses its importance in our quest for our right work. The power of self-trust is truly transformational and can make the difference between a life of greatness and one of mediocrity. For example, the feeling of unworthiness that many of us experience comes from our lack of self-trust and from our ignorance of the fact that we are an essential part of the human race with specific tasks to accomplish. If, on the other hand, we truly believe in our right, and even in our necessity, to be here, the timbre of life changes. For instead of chasing after dreams of financial and personal security, we will be concentrating our efforts on discovering exactly what our special task is, and then pursuing it.

For, as Emerson teaches, you *must* work at this task in order to be happy and successful. Sound realistic? You may not think so, especially if you are trapped in an unsuitable career because of financial responsibilities. Obviously, if you have a family who depends upon your salary, or any other major financial obligations, you cannot just run off to Tahiti, like Paul Gaugin, to paint the natives. Although Gaugin's desertion led him directly to his right work, he probably could have fulfilled his purpose by remaining with his family in France, (though we'll never know.)

You can begin working at your right work a little bit at a time. Obviously, you cannot go from being a banker to a world-renowned chef in a week, or even in a year. But you can enroll in a cooking class or buy a series of cookbooks. When I started writing seriously, I sometimes worked at jobs I hated—a technical editor at a computer firm for one—but always with a purpose, to help me with my writing or just to pay the bills. Either way, I made sure I spent part of my free time practicing my skills by writing. On some days, that meant writing in my journal, on others, working on an article. Regardless of what form it might take or what job I was involved in, I pursued my love of writing, whether on my lunch hour, in the evening, or, whenever possible, during the day.

Eventually, as my articles sold and finally my book, I was able to work at writing more and more. Yet, all this took almost seven years. Why even now, I am still not in the financial position to leave my teaching job which sustains me through the ups and down of a writing career. However, I am now able to spend more time doing the work I love most and less at other jobs.

Let's go back to that friend of mine, who insisted that she couldn't change her position because of financial responsibilities. The truth is, she didn't want to give up the lifestyle to which her six-figure job entitles her. If she really wanted to find her right work, she would gladly have given up a vacation or two to get to it. Her fears, like the fears of many others, have more to do with maintaining a certain lifestyle than survival.

If you read the biographies of famous people, you will often find that they sacrificed luxury and comfort in order to work at what they loved. I remember reading that Alex Haley left a government job in order to make his dream of a writing career come true. This choice caused his standard of living to drop significantly, but he continued, committed to his dream, and eventually found fulfillment by writing *Roots*.

You don't have to make as drastic a change as Haley did. But you could give up a bowling night to take a business class, forgo a few luxury items to pay for your first architectural course, or cut down on your phone bill in order to take singing lessons. Whether the sacrifice involves time or money, you can be sure that if you work—even a little bit—at your right work diligently and consistently, the rewards will offset the sacrifices and you will be led ever closer to fulfillment.

As Emerson says, we only need to "work in the right direction." If we focus on how long it will take to work solely at our task in life, we will certainly never begin, or will quickly become discouraged and give up.

Obsession with a future goal only inhibits performance in the present and leads us farther from fulfilling our purpose. If we remember that the process is just as important as the goal, the moments we spend working at our task will fulfill us as well.

Our true purpose is served when we work fully at our life's task every step along the way. If we can do this, we will find success and fulfillment hidden behind every move we make in the right direction—toward our right work.

Money, Money, Money

Every man is a consumer, and ought to be a producer. He fails to make his place good in the world, unless he not only pays his debt, but adds something to the common wealth. Nor can he do justice to his genius, without making some larger demand on the world than a bare subsistence. He is by constitution expensive, and needs to be rich.

—"Wealth"

After all I've written, you might assume that Emerson discouraged wealth and encouraged poverty. After all, if we follow our natural inclinations when deciding upon a career, then money might not necessarily be important. However, although Emerson would never suggest that we choose our path based on financial remuneration alone, he insisted that the abundance of the Universe is more than available to all of us.

He knew the rigors of poverty in his youth, when he and his family survived mainly on charity. From this experience, he developed the self-reliance and character that would later make him immortal. For poverty, when used as a temporary means for growth, can indeed forge inner spiritual strength and knowledge.

But after we've accepted its gifts and understood its mysteries, it can and should be discouraged as a determinant of one's lifestyle.

When poverty came to me after my divorce, I resented it at first, until I read Emerson's essay "Considerations by the Way," in which he said, "The wise workman will not regret the poverty and solitude that brought out his working talents." And so instead of working against me, my financial state inspired me to begin the career I now enjoy today. Motivated by lack of money and an uncertain future, I used my financial problems as a lever for personal, spiritual, and creative evolution.

Poverty also taught me many things I could never have learned in any other way. First of all, I realized how little one could actually live on and still be happy. I also discovered an incredible joy within myself during those years; it helped me to truly understand that money and material things do not necessarily equal happiness. I went for years without buying any new clothes, but instead of feeling deprived, I learned that beauty has less to do with what you wear and more to do with who you are. And gradually, as the lessons of poverty worked their magic and achieved their purposes, I began to believe that more was possible, as well as desirable.

Emerson writes that one of nature's "iron laws" is that we must, by our own efforts, work our way out of any impoverished state with integrity and with direction. He further explains that nature herself will taunt and torment us until we can reach that point of financial independence and creative fulfillment. In my own case, I found that various monetary and career setbacks obstructed my path until I truly committed myself to my purpose, which meant spending more time writing.

Rather than perceiving such setbacks as negative, Emerson would call them life's way of forcing us to use our talents and to fulfill our potentials. Even our material desires can fire our conviction to succeed and can further spur us on to the achievement of our purpose. When we see something we want, whether it be a better way of life, a vacation, or a new house, our commitment deepens and our efforts increase. Rather than seeing this as accidental or harmful, Emerson knew that even our desires can be catalysts for change and growth.

Still, if greed or fear supply our motivation, rather than the fullest expression of our potential, our spiritual life dries up as materialism reduces everything to matters of power and money. To Emerson, wealth means more than a roof over our heads and food in our mouths or concrete possessions. He equates wealth with freedom—to travel, to enjoy the best company, to avail ourselves of the latest technologies, to appreciate the arts, and to obtain whatever we need to fulfill our destiny.

What I've noticed is that the more I live and work at my purpose, the more my wealth increases. Although my salary has increased as well, I am always aware that my "wealth" includes far more than money, far more than achievement. Wealth has come in many forms, from a friend's assistance to the love of my husband. Nonetheless, Emerson himself recognized that money, if used correctly, can enhance your life and contribute to the evolution of your particular genius.

His rule of thumb is to "spend after your genius." I find that whenever I quote this line, it sparks a lively discussion about what exactly Emerson meant. I believe he means us to use our intuition, that infallible guide, to govern our spending habits. Most of us, I'm afraid, let the ego do our shopping, and we spend money on things that our higher self would never buy. Remember, the ego is concerned with appearances and with power, it thrives on one-upmanship. It wants that new deck because all the other neighbors have one, and it wants that new car to impress family and friends. If we buy with these questionable motives in mind, we may create a substantial amount of debt, while our deeper needs remain unfulfilled.

When we let our intuition control the spending, however, we purchase only those things which resonate with our deepest character. And although those may include a brand new car, the motivation for the purchase will be vastly different than if our ego did the buying. If we buy new clothes, it will be only those that truly express ourselves. With our intuition at the reins, we needn't worry about overspending for it is completely free of any self-destructive energy. Our ego, on the other hand, has a dark underside that often works against our best interests. Just look at all the people who are in debt because of the spending sprees their egos took them on.

"Spend after your genius" could also refer to that part of us involved with fulfilling our purpose. Because we have many inner aspects, some of which may be in conflict, we need to rely on our "genius" for help in financial matters. Connected with our intuition, this aspect of ourselves possesses an inherent consciousness of what we are meant to do in life.

When we let our "genius" guide our spending for us, we are likely to purchase things that enhance our talents and abilities or facilitate the completion of our real work. In a writer's life, a computer would fit nicely into this category, as would the development of an office or a separate room for working. A trip abroad—to study the great buildings of antiquity—might greatly add to an architect's already burgeoning talents. And a food processor might help a busy mother to prepare healthier meals for her children. With all of these purchases, the intention and purpose behind the spending can make all the difference between a life of increasing wealth and one of diminishing resources.

When facing financial struggles, if we unite ourselves with our Godself and work from that, spend from that, and live from that, our lives lose their impoverishment on every level. And when this happens, we may also find ourselves moving toward the wealthy and abundant life we were born to have. Whether that means money in the bank, cars in the garage, or a cabin in the woods, we need always remember to keep the focus on our spiritual life, knowing that if that is taken care of, everything else will be, as well. For as Christ said, "Seek ye first the kingdom of God, and all else will be added."

· 6 ·

The Sixth Secret

Transform Your Intimate Relationships

We must be our own before we can be another's.

—"Friendship"

John Bradshaw once said, "Show me a happy person and I'll show you someone who is not in a relationship." Although Bradshaw was referring to romantic attachments, his observation could apply to friendships and familial relationships as well. After all, isn't it our relationships that wound us, confound us, torment us, and just plain annoy us? And yet, on the other hand, isn't it those same relationships that uplift us, warm our hearts, and make life worth living?

To deal with the paradox, Emerson throws us back upon ourselves with the knowledge that transformation always begins at home. For before we can really experience the incredible depth, joy, growth, and love that relationships can bring into our lives, we must, as Emerson says, "become our own."

One of the most popular clichés of the last decade or so is the idea of "becoming our own person." The truth is, very few of us ever really break free of our dependence on friends, family, and lovers.

See if you can recall how many times you let a friend's opinion take precedence over your own. What if he or she didn't like your particular hairstyle, and you did? Did you accept the disapproval with equanimity, and still feel pleased about your choice? Or did you worry that you had really diminished your appearance, then spend the day brooding about that fatal hair mistake? If you are like most of us, your friend's opinion would have affected you more than you would like.

And the opinions of family members always carry a particular sting to them, because of our learned dependence on approval. After all, since infancy, we are trained to seek out that smiling, nodding face and to avoid the face of disapproval or disdain. We soon learn to savor applause and to dread criticism. When we are praised for being good little boys or girls, our psyches respond to that positive reinforcement and want more of it. And when we are criticized for doing wrong or for going against our family's wishes, the psyche responds to that negative reinforcement by always seeking to please others.

The "disease" of people-pleasing kills more relationships than neglect does, for as long as we allow others' reactions to control us, we are caught in a web that inhibits true communication and prevents real intimacy.

When we are concerned with the opinions others have of us, we only allow what we think "they" want to see and hear to emerge. We keep the real self hidden, while we allow the false self to converse, commingle, and relate to others. In many cases, we detest the "real" us, fearing that the deep self is unlovable.

For most of my life, I feared that if my real self "got out," people would see how really horrid and screwed up I was. So I developed a false self, which I felt would give people what they wanted—or in rebellious times, what they didn't want—and I let that be the face I lived most of my life behind. Many of my relationships during that period were steeped in drama and destruction, which made for quite a bumpy ride through life. My real self emerged at times as well, adding rare moments of beauty to otherwise turbulent relationships.

Finally, using Emerson's guidance on authenticity and self-reliance, I began to chip away at uncovering my real self, while gradually letting go of the facade. Much to my surprise, the more authentically I expressed myself, the better my relationships became. Old friendships either died or renewed themselves, while new ones of incredible dimensions entered my life. Certain familial relationships were healed, while others seemed to lose their power to upset me. And my romantic relationships, through struggle and great learning, finally evolved to the point where I could enjoy the wondrously magical marriage I have today.

An unexpected benefit of my commitment to authenticity was an increase in my self-reliance. In some ways, a rebirth was taking place within me, one that would eventually help me to evolve to the point where I could generate my own happiness, approval, and fulfillment from within.

This self-reliance gradually enabled me to reclaim my real self and to totally transform my life. Step by step and day by day, I revealed more of my self to myself and to those around me. Believe me, challenges and heartaches did arise, but the rewards ultimately proved greater than the hardships. One of the greatest of those was the depth and intimacy that developed in relationships that would have previously been hollow due to superficiality or neediness or dependency.

When we finally learn to "be our own," we can be in relationships out of choice, rather than out of need. Because we aren't dependent on others for approval, acceptance, or love, we find we can interact freely with everyone. Because we are able to live life alone, we are free.

Like me you probably know lots of people who go from relationship to relationship, simply out of the fear of being alone. Unable to satisfy their own needs, they stalk their prey like hungry animals, hoping to find someone who can satisfy their longings. What usually happens is that they are with someone for a while, but then old patterns and problems present themselves, so they go off on the hunt again.

A woman who was about to embark upon her fifth marriage admitted to me that she couldn't stand to live one day without a man. When each marriage was in trouble she started scoping out available men so that she could have someone to fill the void immediately after her divorce. At first, the new man would seem like a dream come true; he wouldn't exhibit any of the negative characteristics of her former husbands. But after a while, he would start treating her exactly as her exes had. Then the fights would begin, over the same issues, activating the same wounds that just seemed to deepen and deepen after each marriage.

A string of failed marriages and painful relationships is not a punishment from God, but a clear-cut message from the Universe to wake up and become whole. For pain, and even abuse, in relationships can show us our wounds and weak spots so that we can heal them.

Ralph, a friend of mine, told me he used the patterns in his own romantic life to help him discover what fears and wounds were keeping him from having what he wanted—a healthy and loving relationship. After several of his romantic ramblings ended in the same way, subsequently bringing up the same pain, he finally looked at how he was contributing to this pattern. "After all," he said, "it isn't a coincidence when you have five consecutive relationships with the same type of woman." He told me that when he finally discovered and—through therapy— healed the wounds that kept him locked in these destructive liaisons, he finally freed himself and for the first time in his life, felt completely whole without a woman.

When we finally "become our own," we can enter into the healthy relationship we have always dreamed of. Only then can we fully experience the joy and intimacy of a relationship based on wholeness and choice, rather than fear and neediness. With wholeness at the helm, our relationships are transformed because of commitment to the most important relationship of all— the one with ourselves.

The Key to Friendship

> The only way to have a friend is to be one.
>
> —"Friendship"

Laura constantly complains about her lack of friends. "I never seem to connect with anyone," she moans, "or if I do, they fade away before I know it. I guess I'm just so unique I can't find anyone on the same level."

I'd noticed that our friendship had deteriorated into a relationship in which I now provided Laura with a sounding board and therapist whenever she felt the need. During the earlier years of our friendship, it had been different, for at that time we had enjoyed real communication with each other. By real communication I mean the open exchange between two people who are sincerely interested in each other. Since those early days, Laura had changed, becoming so focused on herself she had no time for others' input. Which brings me to the core of her problem: she has no interest in anyone but herself.

Rarely does she inquire, or show any interest, about anything going on in my life. And whenever I interject anything about me, she ignores it and immediately refocuses the conversation on her.

Totally absorbed with themselves, people like Laura hardly have any room in their minds or hearts for anyone else. They honestly don't understand why they lack friendships, because they haven't grasped the truth in Emerson's statement that "the only way to have a friend is to be one." Remember, the law of compensation states very clearly that we can only receive what we give. Friendship—like money, love, and respect—needs to be lived out daily. When we are a friend to someone, we care about that person's thoughts, interests, problems, joys—about anything and everything in his or her life. And to show we care, we make sure to listen whenever a friend speaks to us.

As a matter of fact, listening, a lost art, is a primary ingredient in any successful relationship, for without it, we never really get to know another person. Listening creates an environment in which we can feel safe and at ease with someone, knowing that what we say is being heard, considered, and responded to. To truly interact with another, your mind must be engaged, your heart open, your spirit willing. With all these factors operative, you can experience the intimacy of a great friendship. If you don't listen, but instead focus on yourself or on others in the room, no connection is made and no intimacy develops.

Of course, listening is only part of the equation for transforming your intimate relationships. You also have to be willing to communicate honestly.

Emerson emphasizes the importance of honesty in human relationships, a sincerity completely free of flattery, hypocrisy, or any other politely convenient stretching of the truth. "White lies" are unnecessary. Although he does not advocate hurting anyone, he does suggest that you respect the friendship enough to insist on honest and free communication. For example, if a friend asks you if you like her dress and you don't, you should answer truthfully, but with kindness. Or if you see someone you love indulging in self-destructive behavior, you must gently but firmly let him know you are concerned about him.

Intimacy, the foundation of all healthy relationships, can never be formed by superficial communication. Just think of all the relationships—whether friends, lovers, spouses, or family members—you already have in which you don't really know the other person. Unfortunately, most of my family relationships fall into this category; it's often more difficult to open up to relatives because of long-established patterns and emotional baggage. But friendships, mainly because they are chosen, give us the opportunity to create wonderful and close ties. The problems we have in doing so are within ourselves, for we carry our dysfunction with us everywhere.

One of the major problems people suffer from is the fear of intimacy. And because we can't have deep and real relationships without this essential ingredient, it is crucial to understand and conquer this fear.

The reasons for it are numerous. For example, growing up in a nonintimate environment can leave us unfamiliar and uncomfortable with intimacy. Past hurts can prevent us from opening up, as well, because we fear that if we allow ourselves to be vulnerable, we will be hurt again. In essence, however, what these and countless other reasons point to is a fear of exposure.

Because many of us see ourselves as flawed and somehow deficient at the core, we try to live our lives wrapped in the protective armor of personality. Always on guard, we cautiously feel our way through relationships, taking our cues from the other person, careful not to let the "real" us be exposed.

As we develop self-reliance and move toward authenticity, this inner core gets strengthened and begins to feel its way into the outside world. It may take a leap of faith to believe that exposing ourselves to other human beings will lead to healing. But when we do just that, we often discover that people respond to us in wondrous and loving ways.

I am so glad that I've gradually allowed my inner, vulnerable self exposure to the scrutiny of human interaction. Whether by revealing my feelings, stating my opinions, or sharing a perception, my inner self has grown much more accustomed to truth than to lies. Each time I take a stand for what I really feel and allow my vulnerability to show through, my inner character gets strengthened.

For true strength comes from the free expression of who we really are. People who hide behind defenses or false selves remain weak inside, no matter how many bold and brave acts they perform. Real courage is measured by how easily we can open our hearts to others, without fear and without confusion. When we lose our fear of being vulnerable, we can then enjoy deep and meaningful relationships. Intimacy flourishes as we truly relate to those who before might have remained strangers.

Lovers and Other Strangers

> Give all to love;
> Obey thy heart;
> Friends, kindred, days,
> Estate, good-fame,
> Plans, credit, and the Muse,—
> Nothing refuse.
>
> —from the poem
> "Give All To Love"

As a rule, romantic love connotes passion rather than reason, neediness rather than independence, and pain rather than joy. Most of the stories that pay homage to love are tragic in their tone, describing rare moments of ecstasy and peace within a dramatic whirlwind. Judging by the popularity of these stories—just look at our obsession with soap operas—it seems that this is the kind of love we want. Yet there is another—romantic, yes, passionate, yes, but painful, rarely—and it can offer us far more than we ever imagined.

When I was growing up, I was often absorbed in tales of unrequited love, lost love, illicit love, forbidden love, misdirected love, every kind of love except fulfilling love. Weaned on stories like *Wuthering Heights, Gone With the Wind,* and *The Scarlet Letter,* I spent most of my youth searching in dark corners for mysterious and brooding heros, like Heathcliff; or pining over unavailable and unsuitable types, like Ashley Wilkes; or chasing after the frightened and emotionally disabled types like the Reverend Dimmesdale. I knew that this was love for songs, movies, and books painted it so.

After many painful and disappointing romances, I finally got wise to myself. Why this isn't love at all, I thought, but some distorted picture. After that realization, I started the hard work of healing my wounds and diminishing my neediness; in essence, I fell in love with myself. Not in an egotistical way, but in a gentle nurturing way, that encouraged me to flourish, rather than to flounder. "Marianne," I would say, "stay away from those relationships that will inevitably hurt you, and seek out those who will love and cherish you."

But did this new resolve mean I should withhold my feelings in my love relationships or that I should put a lock on my heart until I knew it was safe to come out? And should I refrain from giving, whether it be love, understanding, a friendly ear, or a sports jacket? No, I thought, for I knew that withholding only gets you the same. I decided not to let the new men in my life pay for all my past pain, and not to make myself suffer by damming up the channels of my heart.

At the other extreme, did this decision mean that I should give until I had nothing left, not even myself? Obviously not, for a strong sense of self must be maintained or identity will be lost. Yet what many of us do in relationships is block intimacy by withholding ourselves or weaken it by giving our souls.

When locked in one of these romantic clutches, most of us consider the source of our happiness the other person. If that person loves us, we are happy, if not, we are sad. Given the importance of self-reliance, it's easy to see the folly of this type of behavior, which virtually makes us a slave. Remember, self-reliance is the key to fulfillment, and nowhere is it more important than in romantic relationships, for we are always in danger of losing ourselves to the other person.

When Emerson instructs us to "Give all to love," he means to give freely while still maintaining your identity. Although this may seem paradoxical in theory, it is not in practice. For we really cannot give anything to others that we do not possess. If we don't love ourselves, we cannot love others. If we don't respect ourselves, we can't respect others. We can't express compassion to another, unless we first feel it for ourselves. And we can't give ourselves to anyone, unless we are secure in our self-reliance and identity.

When we possess this inner security, which is based on our connection to God, we can pour out the contents of our hearts, souls, and minds to another, and not deplete ourselves of resources. As a matter of fact, when we possess ourselves, giving to another only enhances our already bountiful inner life.

The main difference between my present relationship and those of my past is that I entered into this one knowing that my happiness comes from within, rather than from without. Not that my husband doesn't add to my happiness, for he does, and in many wonderful ways. But because of my ever-developing self-reliance, I can give freely to him without expecting—or demanding—the same in return. For my foundation lies within the divine wholeness of my being, which keeps me filled instead of empty. This "fullness" enables me to open up my heart to him, secure in the strength of my vulnerability, leaving me unafraid to shower him with more love than I ever expressed to anyone. And the more I express my love, without fears or hidden agendas, the more love I receive and the more loving I become.

What I do expect is to be treated kindly. For example, in my past relationships, I found that I accepted abuse—in my case, emotional—from the men in my life when I didn't love myself. As a matter of fact, accepting it reduced my self-esteem and contributed to my self-hatred. I found, however, that when I finally broke the cycle and put a stop to the abusive behavior and to the relationship, my self-esteem rose as I gradually began my journey back to self-respect.

Although difficult to reflect upon now, I remember putting up with all sorts of abusive behavior from my ex-husband during the dissolution of our marriage. Intermittently, he would take off for weeks at a time, not let me know where he was, and then come back, begging me to take him in again. Because my self-esteem was low, and my self-love barely existent, I welcomed him back each time, even though I knew he was having a affair. Frightened of being alone, I engaged in numerous schemes to "get him back," while my excessive neediness seemed to push him farther away. Eventually, though, the pain and frustration forced me to file for a divorce, but only after a year or more of tumultuous living.

Looking back, I realize that if my inner self had been more developed and less wounded and needy, I would have saved myself a lot of pain. The journey up from that romantic mess was a long one, in which I not only needed to rebuild my tattered life, but also my fragmented self. Luckily, I determined that the "weak" links would have to be strengthened and the hole in my heart filled, not by a man, but by myself, before I could really enjoy the fruits of a truly healthy and fulfilling relationship.

Developing one's inner self to this point doesn't mean that you won't experience any hurt within your relationships, just that the hurt will originate more from conflicts than from abuse or neglect. Also, when resting in self-fulfillment, you won't taint and strangle your relationship with neediness. For when you need another human being for your emotional well-being and survival, you are in a very real way at that person's mercy.

Simply stated, as long as you require another human being to supply your happiness and make up for your lack of self-reliance, you can never truly enjoy a fulfilling relationship. With a strong sense of self, however, you have the chance to create a relationship in which you can give all to love without losing a thing.

Beginnings and Endings

> Yet it is affinity that determines which two shall converse.
> Unrelated men give little joy to each other; will never suspect
> the latent powers of each.
>
> —"Friendship"

What is it that brings us into relationship with another person? Is it physical appearance or personality? Or is it what Emerson calls "affinity," that something similar between two people that draws them together? And if it is that something similar, then is it our interests, our background, or our intelligence level that does the drawing?

Rather than accept the idea that opposites attract, Emerson believed instead that like attracts like. There seems to be a force, a magnetic pull, that compels those of like mind—or soul—into our lives. Ernest Holmes, the founder of the Science of Mind philosophy, was greatly affected by Emerson's ideas, especially this one, which he called "the law of attraction." Eventually, Holmes's ideas were organized into a spiritual philosophy called Religious Science, with churches throughout the world.

Throughout his many metaphysical writings, Holmes speaks about this magnetic force by stating that each of us is surrounded by a "thought atmosphere," which acts like an energy field. Composed of our conscious and unconscious thoughts, this field draws to itself those people, events, and things that resonate with it. Using this model, we can see that through our "thought atmosphere" we are continually either attracting or repelling, for those things that are unlike us will not be drawn into our lives.

Our "thought atmosphere" plays a major role in determining our level of consciousness, the primary magnetizing force in our life. Consciousness, although a difficult term to define, refers to our particular "mindset," which includes the combination of our beliefs, thoughts, and level of spiritual development. Christ lived at an extremely high level of consciousness, while Hitler existed at a very low one. As a matter of fact, the higher we go on the consciousness scale, the more loving and godlike we become, for as we ascend the rungs, we come nearer and nearer to living in total oneness with God.

Those of us with lower levels of consciousness tend to know fear and worry more, while those of us with higher levels rest firmly in faith. Higher levels also tend to fulfill their potential more easily than lower levels, who often sabotage and inhibit their progress. In any event, consciousness plays a large part in the game of like attracting like, for it draws to itself those with matching consciousnesses.

My ex-husband and I shared some surface similarities, as well as some surface differences. But the real pull came from what lurked beneath the surface. For although we both wore a facade of self-confidence and sophistication, underneath it all, we were filled with self-hatred, insecurity, and shame. We also shared a host of addictions; including alcohol, caffeine, food, and romance. I am not talking about being romantic, but about an obsessive romantic bent which seemed to color everything with just the right amount of illusion, making reality practically nonexistent. No wonder we drew each other like magnets, for our wounds and weaknesses were so perfectly matched.

But wounds are not the only forces within us with drawing power. Talents and positive qualities also energize us with the power of attraction. For example, my ex-husband's artistic sensibility was a perfect match for mine.

In some relationships it may be difficult to see where the similarity resides, and what parts of ourselves are being reflected to us by the significant people in our lives. After all, we all know couples who seem so dissimilar that they fit the criteria for the theory opposites attract more than like attracts like.

Let's take a hypothetical case of a woman who seems the complete opposite of her husband. He's a tyrant, she's a pussycat. He's a skinflint, she's a spendthrift. He's intelligent, she's seems intellectually deficient. He's controlling, she's not. In this particular case, where is the evidence for the argument of like attracts like?

Well, as in many areas in life, we need to look beneath the surface to see where the magnetic pull of similarities is operating.

Perhaps the woman, who is far from a tyrant with other people, is a tyrant to herself. Perhaps she pushes herself unnecessarily, and never feels that she can "do enough." And perhaps the tyrannical husband has a weak little boy inside of him that the tyrant is meant to squash, as with his passive wife. The husband's apparently superior intelligence may be compensation for his insecurity in that area, while his wife's seeming lack of intellect may not be a lack at all, but just the result of an erroneous self-evaluation. And maybe deep down, they are both controllers, though they show it in very different ways. The wife may only try to control her temper and her true feelings, while the husband may exercise his control with others more than with himself.

When I look at my present set of friends, I see a vast array of different tastes, lifestyles, and values on the surface, but a deep level of similarities within their cores. We all are fascinated with self-development, with fulfilling our potentials, and with discovering spiritual truth. Our weaknesses—especially the nonvisible ones—match as well, for we all still battle fear and insecurity from time to time, and we all seem to have a tendency to perfectionism. Beyond the specifics, I would say that we connect because we are at the same level of consciousness. If one of us "shifted that level" either up or down, we wouldn't relate to each other as well.

In the essay "Circles," Emerson explains this phenomenon by the statement "A man's growth is seen in the successive choirs of his friends." For oftentimes, what we perceive as a lost relationship is simply a change in consciousness taking its course.

For instance, when my life was focused on money, possessions, and opulent living, I drew people with the same focus into my life. After I lost all my money, however, and began to develop spiritually, all of these people dropped away. Not with nasty words or dramatic confrontations; they just gradually faded from my life. Whereas before we could chatter on for hours, now we had nothing to talk about.

The more I change, the more my friends change. As my inner self developed and my values shifted, different types of people came into my life. Whereas before I drew lots of insecure and self-destructive types, I now attract more confident and self-actualizing types.

Now this doesn't mean that your friends will change every month or so. For your friends' consciousnesses shift as well, which can create a profound and forward-moving friendship. And certain friendships seem to last in spite of these shifts, because of deep bonds formed on other levels. Others may diminish since the essential likenesses that originally drew you together have decreased.

The dissolution of friendships is, to me, one of the most difficult parts of the spiritual journey, even though the resulting growth is welcome and desired. I have discovered, however, that everyone who leaves my life opens the way for an even more wonderful relationship. Emerson understood this when he wrote "When half-Gods go, the Gods arrive."

When a friend or a lover decides to depart from your life, let that person go, for you will soon discover, as I have, that a better relationship is on its way. And with the arrival of this new relationship will come an appreciation of those who have left, for all of them—if we look deep enough—fulfilled their purpose by helping us learn and evolve to the next level. So instead of looking back with regret, look back with gratitude to those who taught us valuable lessons—sometimes through pain—and who unknowingly spurred us onward to more fulfilling relationships.

Mirror, Mirror on the Wall

> My friends have come to me unsought. The great God gave them to me.
>
> —"Friendship"

When I reflect upon the friendships and the loves of my life, I can't help but feel a great deal of gratitude for the many unique and wonderful people who have shared a part of the world with me. Some of them are still in my life, making it richer by their very presence, while others have faded away, either naturally or painfully. Yet, even the painful relationships have blessed me in some way, for they, like all the others, provided me with opportunities for growth.

The complexities of Universal Intelligence are mysterious indeed, for they weave the strands of our lives together with such purpose and grace, sending us exactly what or who we need to evolve into our fullest potential.

Did you ever wonder why your latest lover just seemed to drop into your life? Yes, the law of attraction brought you together, but for what? To prove its own existence? Or is there some greater purpose?

After my divorce, I sought help from a therapist who listened to me complain about my ex-husband's irresponsibility and about how I found myself involved with yet another irresponsible man. "Why is this?" I asked her. "Are all the men out there irresponsible?" Expecting some sympathy, I was quite disappointed when her response was, "Let me ask you, Marianne, is there any way you are being irresponsible in your life?"

Almost angry, I defended myself by saying I send my bills in early, return phone calls, remember birthdays, and usually keep my promises. "Why I am one of the most responsible people I know," I declared. "Your question just doesn't make sense." But Linda persisted. "Is there any way you are being irresponsible to yourself?"

Then it hit me, a flash of intuition that ran right from my heart and into Linda's ear. "Why, I suppose I am not being responsible to myself because I keep ignoring my impulse to write," I muttered, somewhat ashamedly. "Aha," responded Linda. "And how long have you had these impulses?" I almost choked on the answer, after I realized that I had been plagued by these urges and impulses for about fifteen years, yet had totally ignored them!

While we discussed my irresponsible behavior toward myself, Linda explained that the people in our lives can be used as a mirror to show us where we need to change or to grow. For instance, the irresponsibility of the men in my life was really trying to get me to recognize my own responsibility to myself. Her theory made sense to me, as did her suggestion that I needed to honor my responsibility to my writing if I wanted to attract more responsible men.

That experience marked a turning point for me with relationships, for since that realization, I have looked at the significant people in my life with new eyes. For instance, if I become annoyed with what I see as neglectful and abusive behavior, I first and foremost check it out in my mirror to see if I have been that way with myself or toward another. If not, then I know that I need to address the other person with my problem, for although the mirror technique is a valid self-evaluative tool, there are instances in which we don't possess these undesirable traits. What I often find is, the more upset I am, the more likely it is the problem has some connection with me. This does not mean that the other person doesn't possess the trait(s) as well, just that we need to deal with our problem before we engage in any confrontation.

You may think that just getting rid of the guy—or gal—will solve the problem, but it will not; another person will eventually appear with the same characteristic, though usually in a different form. For example, suppose you keep attracting women or men who want to change you. You know the ones I mean, the ones who love you at first, but after a while want you to behave differently, or dress differently, or get a better job. If you find yourself with a few of these "quick-change artists" in your relationship file, see if any part of you wants you to be different. Perhaps you don't really like yourself, and subconsciously want to change. Or perhaps you have a series of voices from the past in your subconscious that constantly criticize you. In each of these cases, you first need to identify and work with these inner difficulties, either through self-exploration or therapy, until they are resolved. After this inner "healing," you will be properly equipped to handle the outside ramifications of this problem. In any event, the advice is the same, deal with the problem in yourself first, then you will know how to deal with it in another.

If you are lucky, perhaps the person will change miraculously, or will leave your life. If not, your realizations will give you the strength and insight to confront this man—or woman— with your concerns, and to resolve them. Remember, God is always presenting us with opportunities to evolve to higher levels of consciousness. You can be sure that when a problem occurs, especially if it repeats itself, the Universe wants you to heal something within yourself. So, next time you are annoyed with someone, remember to turn the mirror on yourself first.

The Purpose of Romantic Love

> Thus are we put in training for a love which knows not sex, nor person, nor partiality, but which seeks virtue and wisdom everywhere, to the end of increasing virtue and wisdom.

—"Love"

Although romantic love is wonderful in itself, according to Emerson, Nature intended that we learn from it our love of humanity, of God, and of wisdom. When we meet, fall in love, and marry, we embark upon a training for a love that extends beyond that particular person.

Most of us shower an inordinate amount of love and attention upon the object of our desire, while often neglecting others in our lives. We may forgive our lovers for any perceived wrong, while still holding grudges against various friends or family members. We may spend all of our money on our lovers, while some worthwhile charity struggles to survive, or be lavish with our free time, while our children suffer from our absence.

Although it is understandable and natural to immerse yourself totally in the beloved, Emerson suggests that we use the beauty and grandeur of romantic love to open up our hearts to the world. When we do this, we view the whole world as our lover and give it time, attention, and perhaps money, as well. Contentment in romantic love should open our eyes to those places where love is needed, to the neglected child, the lonely friend, or the aging parent. Before we can do this, however, we need to transform our romantic love.

When we first fall in love, we are completely entranced. Often, physical appearance plays a large part in our choice, firing us with incredible desire. We know a deep need for this person, and our happiness depends largely upon whether he or she satisfies our longings. After a while, this first stage of love, moves into a still passionate, but less obsessive stage, where hopefully we see our beloved as more than a body and personality, and catch a glimpse of the indwelling spirit or soul.

You probably know an overweight woman whose boyfriend or husband has threatened to leave if she doesn't slim down. Or you may know a woman whose sexual attraction to her husband depends upon whether he maintains a certain image through dress, employment status, or even the car he drives. In both of these situations, love has not progressed past the early stage of surface appeal, but remains trapped by the ego, which wants a mate who satisfies you and helps you look good.

When you get beyond your ego's vision of a person, you can see someone's soul, his or her heart's secrets, and the purpose behind it all. This vision does not obliterate sensual pleasure; on the contrary, it enhances it by adding a spiritual dimension to the mix. With this ingredient present, we focus less on what our lovers can do for us and more on what we can do for them. In this type of relationship, we are committed to each other's spiritual growth and make choices to empower the spiritual part of our lives.

Too often, we obsess over "how this makes me feel" or "what he can do for me" while neglecting or diminishing our partner's needs and feelings. And while I am not advocating self-denial, I am suggesting that a few times during the day, you take time to consider your mate's interests before your own. For instance, if you constantly need to talk over your problems with an empathetic partner, who listens with love and always tries to help you, try asking him—or her—if you can offer the same service. Often we get so locked into patterns that we forget one person in the relationship does most of the giving, while the other does most of the receiving.

It might also help to meditate from time to time on the spiritual connection between you and your lover. Do you have a purpose within the relationship? Is your love for your partner meant to free him/her to be all they can be, spiritually, emotionally, intellectually, and creatively? Does your love for each other include helping to heal each other's emotional wounds, thereby helping each other become more whole?

When we commit ourselves to loving with a spiritual dimension, our love can easily expand and touch every part of our lives. It can also extend itself, as Emerson says, to a love for virtue and wisdom. As true love heals us, we may naturally feel an impulse to be kinder and to help those in need. Compassion will grow within us, helping us to offer an understanding ear and an empathetic heart to those who are hurting.

I know when I am truly loving my partner in this all-encompassing way, I am moved to express this love in any way I can. Obviously, this does not mean that you love others romantically, but that you extend that spiritual and beneficent part of your love out into the world. For instance, a friend may be in need of some openhearted listening and compassionate reassurance. Or a family member may need forgiveness for a past indiscretion. Or perhaps a colleague is overwhelmed with work and could use some help. In short, wherever you see a place, a person, or a situation that could benefit from some loving care, give it freely and watch your heart grow in love and light.

As your love grows and evolves, so may your love of truth and of the uncovering of it, which is wisdom. Because a spiritually oriented relationship encourages full development of your potential, each of the parties involved will continuously expand their knowledge of each other, of life, and of God. As a matter of fact, a love that reaches beyond the five senses and into the spiritual realm will grace your life in countless ways. For when we look at our intimate relationships as a training ground for greater and greater levels of love, we can transform them from things of the world to things of the spirit.

The Seventh Secret
Aspire Toward Greatness

There is a prize which we are all aiming at, and the more power and goodness we have, so much the more energy of that aim. Every human being has a right to it, and in the pursuit we do not stand in each other's way. For it has a long scale of degrees, a wide variety of view, and every aspirant, by his success in the pursuit, does not hinder but helps his competitors. I might call it completeness, but that is later—perhaps adjourned for ages. I prefer to call it Greatness. It is the fulfillment of a natural tendency in every man.

—"Greatness"

"Greatness" means many things. The word may conjure a list of the famous and the mighty, the talented and the wise, the saintly and the dedicated: people like Martin Luther King, Jr., Gandhi, Albert Einstein, Caesar, Queen Elizabeth, and the Dalai Lama. In sports, we might single out Wilma Rudolph or Michael Jordan; in entertainment, Barbra Streisand or Laurence Olivier; and in life . . . perhaps ourselves?

But how can we include ourselves with those who are labeled great? How can we, who struggle with mediocrity and frustration, even come near to greatness?

In *Webster's Dictionary*, the word "great" denotes something "markedly superior in character or quality." And to most of us greatness connotes an element of superiority, placing some above others. Emerson's idea of greatness, in contrast, has to do with what he calls "completeness." This "wholeness," or self-actualization, is brought about by integrating all the parts of ourselves.

Wholeness may seem elusive. We function as best we can, fragmented beings plagued by disjointed, repressed, and hidden aspects of ourselves, unconscious of our various parts. For example, if we want to learn how to sing, we must fight our insecurities and lethargy. One part of us wants to take lessons, while the other part throws up its hands with thoughts like "What's the use, I'll never be any good anyway." And when we want to spend an intimate evening with a lover, part of us may seek to sabotage the intimacy by bringing up something sure to put out even the most passionate fire. In short, you can have a war going on inside of you when you don't even know the enemy.

It is crucial to recognize that we have unknown energies within us that prevent us from being whole. When we engage in any healing or spiritual work, we help to integrate all of these hidden, and often ignored, parts of ourselves into wholeness. We can accomplish this feat in many ways, such as therapy, meditation, and various other methods of self-observation and exploration. The key, however, is not to try to remove, or exorcise, these seemingly "negative" parts from our psyches. Instead, we need to accept them into our beings. When we do this, the magic of acceptance can go to work and transform these split-off parts of ourselves into positive forces. Obviously, this process is a complicated one, in which we usually need trained professionals to help us. Nevertheless, we can progress on our own by using our own methods of self-reflection and examination.

In her book entitled *Core Transformation*, Connirae Andreas, a therapist, agrees that we need to accept our "negative parts" before we can be whole. This is reminiscent of the "active imagination" exercise described earlier in the book, but Andreas has developed a technique that goes a step farther by asserting that, at their core, our faults want something positive for us. Unfortunately, that original purpose has been so distorted our deficiencies reap only destruction.

To reach the positive intention behind our faults, Andreas suggests that we choose a particular fault or weakness, sit quietly in a meditative state, then begin to ask that part what it wants. We don't need, as in active imagination, to personify the part, but we do need to speak to the part directly. Remember, the answers should come from your intuition and not your mind.

To illustrate, let's say that you suffer from shyness and that you would like to alleviate this problem. As you begin asking this part of you what it wants, it may respond by telling you that you are socially inept and that people don't like you. Instead of being dissuaded by this response, keep the questions going. At this point, you may hear that it wants to keep you safe. So you are getting closer to a positive response. You may also see how this part of you resembles an overprotective mother who wants to keep you from harm. By digging deeper, you may discover that what your shyness really wants is love.

Here you may experience an inner knowing and a peaceful feeling that should alert you to the fact that you have reached the positive intention of this unwanted part of yourself. The next step involves loving your shyness. Because you now know that it wants only good for you, you can accept this part into your being, thereby disempowering its harmful, distorted mode of expression. This is where the transformation begins.

Andreas believes that in order to turn our weaknesses into strengths, we need to understand that at their core, our defects yearn for such things as inner peace, love, oneness, and a sense of being "okay." When we connect with these core states, our faults are transformed into strengths which assist us on our journey to wholeness.

We can augment this process by using a simpler exercise of my own, which has helped me toward accepting my "unacceptable parts." First of all, take a piece of paper and write down all of your positive qualities, as well as your negative ones. Be honest, and be careful not to invent faults that aren't there. When you've finished, take each fault and accept it into your heart. Know that you, like all of us, are a human being on the path to wholeness, and that most of us have a long way to go. With that realization, invite your faults to become part of your journey too. Don't try to push them underground, but keep them with you, knowing that usually only that which is hidden can harm you.

Hiding in the shadows along with these destructive parts of ourselves are many powerful and creative parts, especially our Godself, or higher self. Until this essential part of our being is integrated into our conscious life, we cannot function at full capacity. Without this connection, our intuition may be crippled, our capacity for moments of spiritual ecstasy diminished, and our heart nearly paralyzed from lack of divine energy.

Certain talents and abilities may also be hidden from our sight. Whether they were never developed, or someone or some event in our past caused them to run for cover, we owe it to ourselves to unite all the wondrous and exceptional parts of ourselves into the greater whole. For example, perhaps you began your life with a rich array of emotions and delicate sensibilities. If you were in a family that discouraged emotional expression, that side of you probably became repressed so that you could adapt to your environment. Or perhaps you stifled your intelligence because in grammar school you were laughed at by your peers for exceptional academic performance. Regardless of what positive quality we repressed, we need to free these treasures before we can operate at full capacity.

This may prove a bit challenging because many of them are still undeveloped. In other words, our hidden talents and abilities may be "diamonds in the rough," needing practice and nurturing in order to come into full bloom. What we can do, however, is go back over our life, as we did with the exercise in chapter five, and see if we can discover inklings of emerging talents that were subsequently buried. Your intuition will help you to discern a real talent from an imagined one, as will certain awards or commendations from others.

As soon as we begin integrating the rejected and buried parts of ourselves, we will notice a new strength emerging from within us. Emerson's writes that greatness results when all the parts of ourselves work in unison. In recognition of our humanness, however, he realized that total "completeness" takes a long time. By saying that it may be "adjourned for ages," he offers the possibility that the journey may take us beyond this lifetime as well. Rather than be discouraged, we should understand that each step we take toward wholeness is a step closer to greatness. And if we look at true greatness as a continuing process, we can achieve it just by being engaged in the spiritual journey, which is, essentially, the journey to wholeness.

Calling greatness "the fulfillment of a natural tendency in every man," Emerson clearly states his belief that we all have the potential for greatness. All we have to do is commit ourselves to developing our highest nature and then take the steps we need along the way. These may include such things as discovering and fulfilling our purpose, opening our heart, listening to our soul, and anything else that allows our inherent Divine Nature to emerge.

With this type of greatness, we don't necessarily need worldly recognition or remuneration, but only the joy and fulfillment that come from living life at our fullest capacity. According to Emerson, at our deepest level we all desire to win this prize, in order that we may truly know ourselves, truly express ourselves, truly fulfill ourselves, and, in so doing, truly experience the divine energy of which we are a part.

Self-respect

Self-respect is the early form in which greatness appears.
—"Greatness"

In "Greatness," Emerson describes certain types of people he would consider great, such as those who can maintain their opinions even in the face of stiff opposition, and those who would refuse a reward for helping you, whether it be for finding your purse or for saving your life. In these two examples of greatness, as well as others like them, Emerson refers to something unique and noteworthy within such individuals, which he calls "self-respect."

When most of us do something wonderful or exceptional, we expect some kind of recognition from others. For example, if we achieve a much-awaited goal, we enjoy the attention and the praise that usually comes our way. As a matter of fact, sometimes the applause feels better than the accomplishment itself. And when we do a favor or a kindness for someone, we expect an appropriate amount of gratitude. Prominent contributors to charity seek approbation from others, and often achieve great notoriety because of their generosity.

But what about the man or woman who gives for the sake of

giving, achieves for the sake of achieving, and is kind for the sake of being kind? According to Emerson, this person possesses the rarest type of self-respect; his or her self-image is not dependent upon the praise or recognition of anyone.

As children, we learn early that praise feels good and that condemnation feels bad. When we do something wrong, our parents scold and reject us, which causes us to fear that their love, which we depend on so much, may be taken away. When we do something wonderful, we often get praised and rewarded, which makes us feel loved and secure.

As we grow up, hopefully we develop a sense of independence and self-reliance, and learn to rely on our own assessment of ourselves, rather than on others'? Unfortunately, many of us remain in a childish state, searching for recognition around every corner. If we have a party, we want to hear how much fun it was. If we wear a new dress, we can't wait to hear other people tell us how beautiful it is. If we achieve any type of success, we expect praise and may even solicit it when it is not forthcoming.

Of course, there is nothing wrong with praise in its purest form; letting people know how special they are, and what a wonderful thing they've done, is natural and loving. But what if we become so dependent on other people's reactions that we don't know if we are acting for ourselves or for others? When we are free of this need for praise, we can think, act, and speak from our truth, without any thought of whether others will notice or not.

I remember hearing an actor say that because she was not attached to the praise she received, she was free from the criticism as well. But when we need approbation from others, we become vulnerable to critics; our self-esteem moves up and down depending on what type of commentary we are receiving.

For instance, let's say that you are the actor who has just appeared in a play, reviewed by two different critics. While reading the first review, your self-assessment shoots way up at seeing comments like "extremely talented," "magnificent craftsperson," or "stellar performance." While reading the second one, however, your self-esteem plummets at the words "exuding as much charm as a dead fish." But which is the accurate assessment, the positive one or the negative one? Of course, you could continue to seek out more and more reviews to determine whether you are a good actor or not. Or you could look within yourself and produce your own review. Do you think you did a good job?

Of course, constructive criticism can help us with any task or situation. For example, writers depend upon their editors to help them fine-tune their prose. And if a particular outfit detracts substantially from your appearance, a genuine friend will be sure to let you know. However, when you have a strong sense of self, you can learn from what the various positive and negative assessments may tell you, without being elevated or deflated by the individual comments.

Self-respect is the foundation we need to remain centered and secure within ourselves, in the face of criticism or in the face of praise, which are essentially two sides of the same coin.

There is more to self-respect, however, than detachment from the opinions of others. Emerson also describes something he calls a "bias" in each individual, which must be followed for greatness to appear. By bias he means the various interests, talents, desires, and intuitions that point us in a direction uniquely important only to us. It is a mark of self-respect to listen to what he calls this "private oracle" guiding us to our own individual expression of greatness in the world.

Self-respect calls forth the wholeness of our being, rather than fueling our sense of lack. For the more we dig down, touch our wholeness, and bring it to the surface, the more we can hearken to this inner divinity, which will guide us unerringly in the direction of happiness, fulfillment, and greatness.

Courage

Whatever you do, you need courage. Whatever course you decide upon, there is always someone to tell you you are wrong. There are always difficulties arising which tempt you to believe that your critics are right. To map out a course of action, and follow it to an end, requires some of the same courage which a soldier needs. Peace has its victories, but it takes brave men to win them.

—"Courage"

When speaking about greatness, we cannot overlook courage, one of its most essential components. For when we look at great men and women, we see courage as the sustaining rung in the ladder that helped them rise to a higher stature. On the other hand, when we look at ourselves, we often perceive lives controlled by fear and timidity. Yet deep within each being lies the courage we seek, as well as all the other qualities necessary to greatness. The only difference between us and the "great" is that they have uncovered their courage, whereas we have not.

Do you remember the story of *The Wizard of Oz?* The Cowardly Lion joins the trek to see the wizard, hoping he will be given courage. Throughout the journey, the lion shows courage in many ways, but he doesn't feel it until the wizard gives him a "testimonial," or a formal recognition of his bravery. In other words, the lion had exactly what he was seeking within himself all the time, he just didn't know it.

And so it goes with the rest of us. For our courage, like our joy, our talents, our compassion, and our greatness often lies buried within us. We are, all of us, on a kind of treasure hunt, continuously uncovering the wondrous jewels of our being and bringing them into the light of the world.

When we embark upon our spiritual path, obstacles will inevitably mar our progress or deter our advance, and we are called upon to bring forth our courage so that we can heal our fears and our insecurities, and subsequently become more whole.

During a trip to Concord, Massachusetts, a few years ago, I came upon the story of Amos Bronson Alcott, father of Louisa May. Apparently Alcott, who had many innovative ideas for education, spent twenty years landing posts in various school systems from which he was subsequently fired. In spite of all this rejection, he never gave up on his dream of a new system of education, and finally the town of Concord accepted him and his ideas by giving him a permanent post.

When I think of this story, I am struck by Alcott's determination and faith in himself, which eventually netted him a place in history. If he had given up after one, or even a few rejections, he would have never given his gift to the world or fulfilled his own potential for greatness. It is not surprising, then, when we note his incredible courage and faith, that he was a friend and advocate of Emerson and his ideas.

And faith is key to helping us reach our goals and achieve our potential. For without it, courage becomes mere bravado and often loses much of its impact. As a matter of fact, faith builds courage and courage builds faith.

When Christ talks about how faith can move mountains, he reminds us of our inherent divine nature and of our connection with God. For when we have faith we activate the creative power of our being, impelling ourselves to the fulfillment of our goals. Without faith, we live continually with a sense of limitation, doubting ourselves at every turn.

One of the main reasons for failing to reach our potential and realize our dreams is that we give up at the first sign of defeat. Instead of reaching deep within and pulling out the courage we need to move through obstacles, we decide we just don't have what it takes. Then despair sets in and kills any remnant of hope we have left.

When you are weary and despairing and want to give up, try picking up a biography of anyone who ever achieved anything and you will see countless examples of incredible faith and courage in the face of opposition. You might need to allow yourself to really feel the despair before you can step out of it. In other words, instead of denying your fear and hopelessness, let yourself express all the negative things you are feeling. Scream if you like, curse the fates, complain, whatever, but get it all out. You will often find that after this energy is released, a new sense of courage emerges, because we have cleared out the debris, so to speak.

During challenging times, we need to remember that fear and courage often walk together, and that the courageous move forward not because they lack fear but often because of fear itself. This realization can often help us release some of our own fear, now that we understand even the greatest heros of history knew what it meant to be afraid. As Emerson wrote in the essay "Courage," "He has not learned the lesson of life who does not every day surmount a fear."

I know myself that fear often walks beside me and tries to thwart my efforts. Each time I take a step forward or attempt any kind of risk, fear encourages me to stay paralyzed and not move ahead. I remember how frightened I was when I first began teaching a few years ago. I only took the job out of desperation; it was something I always said I would never do, standing up in front of a classroom and speaking to a group of young, impressionable, and often bored faces.

The fearful voices within me told me to quit. They tried to convince me I had nothing to say and worse, I couldn't even say it well. During the first few classes, I barricaded myself behind a pile of books, which I hoped would save me if I couldn't come up with ideas. My body and my voice trembled throughout the early classes. Nevertheless, I kept on teaching until I gradually came out from behind the books, lost my nervousness, and eventually even enjoyed myself! Now I absolutely love speaking in front of groups and would never have missed the opportunity to move through this fear.

Because of this experience, and others like it, I discovered that something wonderful lies on the other side of fear, and that something is power. For when you look fear in the face and move ahead in spite of it, it eventually transforms itself into an inner power which strengthens you for the next challenge. When this happens, your whole being is empowered and charged with divine energy. You feel stronger, more loving, and more alive. Your sense of the God within is enhanced, which gives you a deep feeling of inner peace and well-being. In other words, an incomplete part of you is made whole by moving through the fear, which brings you closer to self-empowerment and integration.

When you connect with this power, courage becomes a constant companion on your spiritual journey rather than an absent friend. And although you still may experience fear, you know that your courage will help you transform it into authentic power. Greatness and spiritual fulfillment are the fruits of this process, which continues on throughout our lifetimes and possibly beyond.

Character

> This is that which we call Character—a reserved force which acts directly by presence, and without means. It is conceived of as a certain undemonstrable force, a Familiar or Genius, by whose impulse the man is guided, but whose counsels he cannot impart; which is company for him, so that such men are often solitary, or if they chance to be social, do not need society, but can entertain themselves very well alone.
>
> —"Character"

Difficulties, we say, will give us character, as will wrinkles on our face and gray in our hair. But does the sheer act of saying that one has character make it so? And more importantly, what does it mean to have character and how do we recognize its presence or absence?

According to Emerson, character is difficult to define, but we know it when we see it or, more accurately, feel it. For a person of character has a certain presence, which often inspires and uplifts us. When we are around someone like this, we are aware of a profound depth and inner strength emanating from them. They seem almost multidimensional. We are conscious of an aspect of this person that goes beyond face, body, and personal qualities, adding a divine dimension to such a being. This dimension often inspires awe in those of us without the same depth of character, while at the same time encouraging us toward greatness.

A person of character doesn't need to speak of his or her greatness and grandeur of soul. It is evident in this person's demeanor, voice, words, and deeds. Men and women of character are secure and self-reliant. They do not need to tell you how great they are, for greatness emanates from them like warmth from a flame.

Emerson also recognizes character as a guide whose wisdom is indispensable to its possessor. This guidance, often obtained in solitude, enables these men and women to be comfortable with, and even seek solitude during certain times in their lives. Complete within themselves, they lack the fear that most people have about being alone. It is as if an "inner character" keeps them company and provides them with direction. For these individuals know the value of solitude for cultivating what the Quakers call the "still, small voice" of the God within. A part of our intuitional system, this "voice" can be heard best when we are alone.

Obviously, many people of character are social and enjoy the company of people. The difference is that they are social out of choice and not out of need. Unfortunately, some folks need the company of others, and seek it as a way to avoid their own. How many times have you heard someone say "I am a people person, I need to be around people"? Often, I would think, for many of us have a rather difficult time being alone and go out of our way to avoid it.

Now, I am not denying the joy and fulfillment others can bring into our lives. As a matter of fact, I consider myself a "people person," having always enjoyed the company of friends. Since I began my spiritual search, however, I've heightened my need for solitude and lost a great deal of my need for people. I still love to be with companions, and my friendships are even more important to me than ever. The difference is, I don't need them to fill a void in my life. For an inner relationship has been developed, which infuses all my relationships with love rather than with need.

When you become intimate with yourself, you dispel that neediness that can contaminate relationships and you begin relating to people in a different way. Instead of wanting something from them, you are more concerned about giving and about sharing yourself with them, which opens the door to relationships that are free of dependencies and games. If you don't develop this intimacy with yourself first, you are destined to seek it elsewhere, while the gold mine within you lies dormant and unexplored.

As with all the other traits of greatness, your unique character lies waiting to be discovered by you and brought to the surface. Rather than being developed, character needs to be uncovered.

And that can only be done by being alone and becoming intimate with yourself. Although it may seem that outside events develop character, the truth is, during difficult times you are just removing the darkness that covers the light.

When you undergo an extremely trying circumstance, such as a death in the family, a divorce, or some other occurrence that has caused you a great deal of pain, you have the choice to numb the grief through social interaction or other outside stimulations—work, working out, drugs, etc.—or to reach the core of it by being alone. If you choose to go within yourself and just "be" with the pain, eventually, as you move though it and out of it, a sense of character will emerge within you to strengthen your soul and enhance your life. On the other hand, if you avoid this inner communion with your pain, your character will not be altered or strengthened, but will actually be diminished, so that each subsequent problem will drain you of inner strength and deprive you of the opportunity for growth. In short, character is formed by dealing directly with our problems, rather than running away from them.

A few years ago, a woman I know named Sarah experienced a tragic divorce, lost custody of her children, and dealt with the death of her mother, all within the same year. I am sure we would all agree that this is enough to cause even the strongest of us to do whatever we could to avoid such harsh realities. Sarah, however, did not run away, although she sought the support of family and friends throughout her tragedy. Instead, she faced the situation, expressed any pain or emotion she felt, and deepened her character day by day.

She spent time alone so she might feel her loss—cry, scream, kick, or shake her fists at fate. Because of her direct, rather than indirect, handling of her grief, she grew stronger, wiser, and even more loving. And what is most amazing, she even forgave her husband for the pain he caused her. If you met Sarah today, you would see a loving, positive person with lots of character and inner strength.

Margo's situation illustrates the other side of the coin.

Bob was Margo's high-school sweetheart, and when they married, she thought the rest of her life would be as idyllic as their previous years together. Unfortunately, Bob started cheating on her almost immediately after their marriage. While she tried to look the other way, steeped in illusion, Margo told all of her friends that her life with Bob was improving with every passing day. The truth, however, was far from paradisiacal, for the more he entertained himself with other women, the worse he treated Margo.

Throughout the mistreatment, which included emotional abuse as well as some minor physical skirmishes, Margo still idolized her husband and even convinced herself that he really loved her in spite of his actions. When friends tried to talk to her, she denied that anything was wrong and, on some level, believed her own lies. Eventually, she relied on tranquilizers as well as alcohol to keep the illusion going, while her marriage deteriorated daily. Finally Bob informed her that he was getting a divorce and intended to marry someone else.

Unable to deal with that harsh reality, Margo wound up in a psychiatric clinic, where, with the help of professionals, she finally began to face the truth about her life, and perhaps to discover her own source of inner strength and to uncover her character. For Margo had the same potential for character development we all have; the difference is that she chose to avoid her problems rather than face them.

During difficult times, we must meet our darkness head-on in order to unearth the character that is already ours. And while human interactions may still console us, we will forge within ourselves a new relationship with the inner self, which can't help but improve our lives. And when this happens, we will be filled with that rare combination of inner strength and power that will catapult us toward greatness.

Heroism

Heroism is an obedience to a secret impulse of an individual's character.

—"Heroism"

I've always loved the opening line of Charles Dickens's immortal novel *David Copperfield:* "Whether I shall turn out to be the hero of my own life, or whether that station will be held by anyone else, these pages must show." Since I read those lines many years ago, I wondered about heroism, what it meant and how it would affect my life. Never in those young days did I think about becoming my own hero, for I always believed that someone else would "hold that station" and would rescue me from all the problems of existence.

For me, as for many young women in years past, meeting the "right man," would be the culmination of the search for the hero. Marry Mr. Right, we thought, our knight in shining armor, and every difficulty, including any inner confusion and torment, would be gone forever. In many of our lives, a string of Mr. Rights would come and go, leaving us with our problems rather than any solutions.

Early in my twenties, I read a passage in a women's magazine that tried to point me in the other direction. Although I can't remember who wrote it, the words still remain in my memory, even after all these years: "Of all the people you will know in your lifetime, you are the only one you will never leave or lose. To the questions of your life, you are the only answer. To the problems of your life, you are the only solution."

I apologize for not remembering the author, and for perhaps altering the words a bit. But I can still feel the powerful effect they had on me—I was a bit rattled and somewhat angry at the declaration that we must work out our own lives, that no one could do it for us.

I don't know whether it was the anger or just the effort involved in taking control of your own life that caused me to ignore these words of wisdom. Or perhaps my romantic side refused to let go of the idea that someday my prince would come. Nevertheless, I eventually relinquished the responsibility for my own life and placed it in the hands of another, whom I thought to be my prince and rescuer.

It was only when this rescue attempt failed disastrously, leaving me with more problems than ever before, that I finally understood: no one could save me but myself. It was then that I began my own heroic journey, which continues to this day.

When Emerson talks about "obedience to a secret impulse," he refers to our heroic journeys; in which we are called mostly by our own intuitions, impulses, revelations, and synchronicities, which seek to awaken us to our potential and bid us to follow their lead. What this journey eventually brings us to is the fulfillment of our destiny, which ultimately leads us to God.

As I discussed in the chapter on finding your purpose, the primary reason for our existence is to discover our oneness with God. This journey, which in my mind is an inward one, has frequently been misinterpreted and misdirected and so has led us in the opposite direction. Through a single misperception, we have placed the source of life outside ourselves and then tried to reach it by means which can only take us farther away from our goal.

Traditional Christian religions are not completely wrong in their theories; it is just that they place God, the devil, and all the glories of heaven and the agonies of hell without, instead of within, where they belong. Granted, all these things are reflected in the outside world, but their sources lie within us, and within the collective of which we are all a part. This single misperception of God as without instead of within, has led many on countless unfulfilled searches and futile quests.

We have pleaded with external Gods for so long that our inner lives have nearly dried up for lack of use. For whether we seek God in churches, in books, or in other people, we always "miss the mark," so to speak. If only we would turn within in the first place, we would save ourselves from the needless obstacles that thwart our progress. For when we know the God within, we then see God everywhere, hidden within the teachings of churches, within the pages of books, and within each human heart.

As Joseph Campbell has well noted, heroic stories function as metaphors from which we extract clues for our own inward hero's journey. The dragons and evil villains of these classic tales point to the darkness that exists within ourselves. And ultimately we must conquer this darkness first, before we can deal with the demons of the world.

For example, I noticed that I often came in contact with domineering women who tried to control my thoughts, my actions, and my impulses. These women appeared either through work or through friendship, and helped me feel inadequate and inferior in whatever I attempted to do. After dealing with three or four of these dragon ladies, I asked myself whether or not a similar energy existed in me, in other words, did I have a controlling, shrewlike person inside of me that sought to demean and humiliate me?

After some reflection, I uncovered a part of myself that could be even more abusive than its outer reflection. This part constantly tormented me with demands and accusations such as, You never do enough, You are lazy, You never work up to your potential, and so forth. It would take my greatest work and reduce it to trash by accusing me of not putting forth my best effort. Nothing I did could ever satisfy this inner tyrant.

After this revelation, I went to work on slaying my demon, for I knew that I needed to transform it before I could deal effectively with its external counterparts. Obviously, this process was neither easy nor pleasant, but the more I continued dialoguing with and understanding this abusive part, the more it dissipated. And as often happens, that negative energy was not only dissipated but transformed; where it once used to diminish, it now discerned and guided. Now, if a controlling woman shows up in my life, which rarely happens, I can deal with her without fear and without intimidation, and can actually use her energy to inspire rather than deflate me.

Each time an obstacle in the outer world threatens to throw me off my course, I immediately turn within, discover the inner counterpart, then heal it in any way I can. This, of course, moves me toward wholeness and enables me to "fight" and transform any problem that I encounter without.

When we avoid this part of the journey, however, and try to rescue ourselves before we really confront the inner demon, we often are led into confrontations—in the outside world—with more frightening monsters than we ever knew before. Rescue attempts from others may also save us from these monsters for a while, but eventually we are thrown back upon ourselves and challenged to take up the real hero's journey. In short, the only way out is through.

Like the monsters, the princes and magicians of legend are forces within us, not without. And it is to these inner energies that we must turn for salvation, not to the ones without. For when you discover that Prince Charming is only a metaphor for an inner resource that exists within all of us, you will then understand the meaning of the fairy tales that so innocently misdirected us.

That is not to say that no help exists in the outside world, for often a person may say just the right thing to us to help us through a difficulty. And through synchronicity, we may stumble upon the perfect book that contains just the message we need to hear. Outside forces might offer financial assistance or help of some kind, from a compassionate talk to a new job. Recognize these helpmates, but also recognize that we must *totally* accept the gift, on all levels, before we can fully utilize it.

For oftentimes, we may receive the advice, read the passage from the book, or even accept the job, yet never really benefit fully from the gift. I think of how, at a young age, I read those profound words about being the answer to my own problems and ignored them. My refusal of this gift cost me many years of suffering which could have been avoided if I had accepted the wisdom of that passage.

But Emerson and I want nothing to do with regrets, for we know that life continually offers us the opportunity to take up our own lance and charge forward—or more appropriately, inward—on our heroic journey. As always, the choice is ours. We simply need to ask ourselves, as did David Copperfield, whether we are the hero of our own lives, knowing that to yield that post to another will lead us farther astray and cause us more problems. So accept help when it is given you, but learn to discern between a rescue attempt and honest-to-goodness assistance that is meant to enhance the journey, rather than deter it.

Mediocrity

> There seems to be no interval between greatness and mean-
> ness.
>
> —"Heroism"

When we see the word meanness, we usually think of something nasty or disagreeable. In this case, however, Emerson
means something of average or mediocre quality. He seems to
say we are either average or great, that no middle ground exists.
Now, we could debate the truth of this statement and argue that
there are gray areas in between. However, we would be best
served if we looked at the mediocrity in our own lives, and reflected upon how it obstructs us from fulfilling the greatness that
is inherently within us.

Let's face it, we live in a mediocre world. We watch mediocre
television programs, view mediocre films, eat mediocre food,
and live mediocre lives. We are satisfied to "get by," and rarely
draw upon our deepest potential. After a while, this type of behavior becomes comfortable, both for ourselves and for society.

A few years ago, I realized I had a "mediocrity contract" with
society: in the past I had made a silent bargain with the world not
to excel too much in any field. Now all this contracting and bar-
gaining went on without any words and without any conscious
knowledge. On some level I understood that my middle-class
background encouraged me to be smart, but not too smart;
pretty, but not too pretty; talented, but not too talented; and
successful, but not too successful.

Obviously, there were always certain people in my life who
wanted me to succeed and who expressed their support. But
beyond these folks lie many expressed and unexpressed messages
that prevent some of us from excelling. Messages such as Don't
get too big for your britches, Who do you think you are anyway?, and Make sure you don't stand out from the crowd,
among others, serve to dissuade us from high levels of achievement. An excessive emphasis on humility and on "fitting in" fur-

thers this programming. And many of us are also told, nonverbally if not verbally, not to "show up" others in our family or community. We also must be careful not to overturn anyone's belief systems. In other words, if your family believes that something can't be achieved, you mustn't show them that it can.

Although excelling may often be encouraged on the surface, somewhere within, our subconscious mediocrity holds the reins. For example, throughout my childhood and young adulthood, I received mixed messages regarding success and thought it best if I toned down my act and my talents instead of fine-tuning and developing them.

So through much of my life, I only allowed myself to reach a certain level, knowing that going beyond that would mean I was betraying both my family and society. Sounds crazy, doesn't it? But, while I'm at it, I'll even take it a step farther, and say that most of us have these contracts.

Just look at how we react when we are near someone who seems "to have it all." Do we admire and want to get to know this person, or are we envious, while trying to discover "the flaw" that we know must be within. No one can be creatively fulfilled, beautiful, wealthy, successful, and happy at the same time! Often, we make people like this feel that they don't belong with the rest of us, instead of trying to discover their secrets so we can apply them to our own lives.

Just a little taste of this type of rejection, either from our family or from society, may be enough to keep us on the mediocrity track for most of our lives. After all, we all know that no one is threatened by mediocrity, and if we want acceptance, we will heed its call rather than allow ourselves to rise to greatness.

Excelling also calls uncomfortable attention to ourselves, which causes many of us to avoid the limelight rather than let our greatness shine. Mediocrity, on the other hand, allows us to remain in the background where the critical eyes of others cannot fall upon us. For example, suppose you've just decided to fulfill your life's dream of becoming an entrepreneur and are opening your own business. By taking this risk and presenting your products in public, you expose yourself and leave yourself open to the judgments of others. While you remained in the background, you were safe, though your talents were hidden.

If you look at those exceptional human beings who have fulfilled their potentials, you will find that many of them receive as much criticism as praise, especially early on in their careers. But something inside them, perhaps a "call to greatness," allowed them to withstand the criticism and reach beyond the barriers of mediocrity. Most of us, however, are bound by the unconscious contract that encourages us to be average and "safe."

If we look at our lives and see that we have only reached a small percentage of our potential in most areas, then we need to reflect upon whether we've swallowed society's—or perhaps our family's—bait and become hooked on mediocrity. Each of us knows in the heart whether or not he or she is operating under this type of internal contract. For example, do you always work below your potential in school or on the job? Do your relationships fall short of what you know they can be? Is your health or appearance far below what it could be? Do you succeed initially and then do something to destroy it? Do you refuse to grasp those opportunities that would really help you succeed? Do you attempt to "tone yourself down" so as not to upset other people? Do you blatantly disregard any attempts at self-development and self-improvement for fear of overshadowing friends, family, or members of the community? Have you become more accepting of mediocrity? Do you even seek to perpetuate it?

When bound by mediocrity, we usually are conscious of an energy inside us telling us that we can do better. In this case, I do not mean that punitive, parental voice saying Nothing is ever good enough, but that gentle, empowering voice that intermittently lets you know you are working below your potential. If you hear this voice, and it doesn't have a parental ring to it, then you can safely bet that it is your greatness calling to you, and encouraging you to follow its lead, instead of the stagnating energy of mediocrity.

But how do we break this contract which has netted us acceptance, safety, and anonymity for most of our lives? The best way I have found is to make a list of all we have lost by heeding mediocrity's call, and then ask ourselves if we want to continue living beneath our potential. How many chances have we lost, how many opportunities have we screwed up, and how many moments of ecstasy have we sacrificed? For mediocrity has nothing to do with ecstasy, enthusiasm, empowerment, or energy of any kind. It is a lack of energy that drains life out of people, makes them old before their time, and takes all the wonder out of life.

If you look around you in the world, you will see what mediocrity has done to most people's lives: the couple dining out who have nothing to say to each other, the friend who can't think of anything to talk about other than the superficial and meaningless, the worker who does the least he or she can while waiting patiently for retirement and for more years of safe and comfortable living.

Greatness has nothing to do with safety or with comfort. It forces us to reach deep within ourselves and to draw upon the gifts, abilities, and power we already have. Mediocrity is a powerful magnet, but living fully can bring us toward the completeness, or wholeness, of which Emerson speaks. And although we may not complete the journey in this life, our commitment to greatness will touch our lives with growth, energy, beauty, and creativity as we move daily toward the fulfillment of our highest potential, and toward truly successful living.

Commencement

Rather than an ending, finishing this book marks the beginning of a new, and hopefully, more fulfilling life. For experience has taught me that these seven secrets have amazing transformative powers, and that they can lead anyone toward real success and happiness. Okay, so where do we begin, and how do we get from where we are to where we want to be?

After reading a book like this, I often feel overwhelmed by the amount of work I need to do. Discouraged by my imperfections and limitations, I almost want to give up rather than begin the grueling task of applying whatever it is to my life. Soon, however, that feeling passes, as I realize one glaring and essential truth: I am a *human* being.

Throughout this book, I have stressed the idea that God resides within us, and that we are, by nature, divine. Yet while that is true, we cannot forget the other side of the coin, namely our humanness. For unlike God, we are both human and divine, and need to honor both sides of our nature. For example, if we meditated for days without eating, most likely our bodies would suffer. Or if we ignored our emotions, while frantically seeking bliss, no doubt we would harm ourselves in some way. And

while there are those "enlightened" individuals who can tran-
scend their human functions, most of us cannot—at least not at
this moment.

Which brings us back to those seven secrets and to what may
seem like an overwhelming task. First of all, accept your humanness, as well as your divinity, and realize that much of what I
write about may take years or even lifetimes to achieve. On the
other hand, enlightenment can happen within a moment or
within a day. Accept the fact that mistakes and setbacks will
occur, along with growth spurts and amazing transformations.
Also be aware that trying too hard may short-circuit the process.

Anthony DeMello, a Jesuit priest, once said, "The world is full
of people who will never change, just because they are trying so
hard to change." Seems contradictory, doesn't it? But if you look
closer, you will see the truth here. For example, have you ever
tried so hard to achieve something that you made more mistakes
than ever? And what about the business executive who has a
heart attack after years of stress or strain? Or an athlete who
strives so hard for the perfect performance that he falls on his
face.

Now I am not saying to just lie back and let the world go by,
for we all know that we need to expend some effort in order to
achieve anything. But what type of effort? In my life, I have
found that what works best when we want change is first and
foremost to accept ourselves the way we are, then to make an
internal decision and commitment.

Okay, so you really want to learn to live these "secrets" and to
enhance your lives. Good. Get clear about what you want, make
sure you really want it, then commit to it with all your being. Do
this quietly, completely, and wholeheartedly but without stress
and strain. Don't try to force anything. Then ask your intuition
and the God within to help you integrate these changes within
your life. Be aware of the principles I've presented and gently and
consciously weave them into your days at whatever pace seems
comfortable to you.

If you notice some resistance coming up, don't try to push it
away. Let any part of you that doesn't want to incorporate any
or all of these ideas have its say. It may reveal some deep-seated

fear of change or of happiness that needs to be dealt with. In that case, use the inner dialoguing techniques I describe in the book to resolve these conflicting parts. However, resistance may also mean that you are not yet ready for the change. Timing is important in spiritual growth, as well as in life. Being sensitive to your inner voices, intuition, and feelings will help you determine if the particular change is right for you at this time.

Furthermore, you simply may not resonate with certain ideas. Remember, the path of self-discovery and self-reliance demands that you choose what you want and leave the rest. My book is no different. Your intuitive heart will guide you as to what "fits" for you and what does not. After all, this is your path, not mine.

Ultimately, however, we need to understand that change is really not the issue here, but that recovery is. And by recovery I don't mean that of the twelve-step variety; I am referring to the recovery of your real and potential self. As I explained in the first chapter, Emerson's ideas serve to bring you back to your self and to the God within. In reality, we are not changing anything but are allowing what is already within us to emerge. But as if we were a sailboat we need to point ourselves in the right direction and then let nature do the rest. Sometimes, we may need to work a bit to keep ourselves on course; proper care and supervision is essential in order to maintain a powerful vessel. Most importantly, however, we need love, both of ourselves and of God. After that, love of others and the world will naturally follow.

I'd like to offer you this book as a possible guide through uncharted waters. Use it as you would any guide, with your intuition at the helm, to lead you toward yourself, toward God, and toward home.